Bjørnstjerne Bjørnson, William Morton Payne

Sigurd Slembe, a dramatic trilogy

Bjørnstjerne Bjørnson, William Morton Payne

Sigurd Slembe, a dramatic trilogy

ISBN/EAN: 9783337304461

Printed in Europe, USA, Canada, Australia, Japan

Cover: Foto ©Andreas Hilbeck / pixelio.de

More available books at **www.hansebooks.com**

SIGURD SLEMBE

A Dramatic Trilogy

BY

BJÖRNSTJERNE BJÖRNSON

TRANSLATED FROM THE NORWEGIAN

By WILLIAM MORTON PAYNE

BOSTON AND NEW YORK
HOUGHTON, MIFFLIN AND COMPANY
The Riverside Press, Cambridge
1888

TRANSLATOR'S PREFACE.

THE work here reproduced is probably the noblest production of a literature which, while neither very rich nor very ancient, still deserves to be better known to English readers than it is. Björnstjerne Björnson, who may be said to have created that literature, still remains its most conspicuous figure, although his later work suffers, artistically speaking, from the too obvious enlistment of the author's genius in the service of political and social reform.

To the majority of English readers Björnson is known solely as the author of a series of charming stories of Norwegian peasant life. These stories have been made familiar by repeated translations into English, from the version of "Synnöve Solbakken," prepared by Mary Howitt in 1858, to the recently published uniform edition of all the stories, which we owe to Professor Rasmus B. Anderson. But to his countrymen Björnson's fame is far from being founded upon these stories alone. He is chiefly great, not as a novelist, but as a lyric and dramatic poet, and in these phases of his literary activity he is practically unknown to English readers. Yet it is impossible to form any adequate estimate of his genius without taking account of his verse as well as of his prose, and of his dramas no less than of his idyllic tales.

Of the long series of dramatic works in prose and verse which he has produced, the trilogy of " Sigurd Slembe " is altogether the finest ; it is characterized by the greatest breadth of treatment, by the most masterly delineation of character, and by the highest poetic truth.

Björnson is the great national writer of Norway because his finer work deals with national themes. His contemporary, Ibsen, endowed with genius of a high order, has chosen to be cosmopolitan rather than national, and so the claim made for Björnson cannot be disputed on behalf of his most famous fellow-worker in the field of letters. Björnson's tales of peasant life are purely national, his more poetic dramas are no less so, and his best lyrics are true northland notes. Norway is peculiarly rich in materials for a national literature. It is, more than any other part of Europe, the home of that rich mythology which has so profoundly influenced Teutonic thought, and which, had conditions been more favorable, might have borne in earlier times a fruitage comparable for poetic wealth with that of the mythology of Southern Europe which so early became embodied in works of imperishable beauty. In Central Europe we find this mythology in a somewhat corrupt and perverted state, modified by classical influences and mixed with elements of indigenous growth. In the North alone did it remain comparatively free from foreign admixture ; there alone did it acquire form and consistency, and there did it wait in vain, until too late, for some master mind to so mould it that it should be sure forever of the world's regard. But the Norsemen had more pressing work at hand than the cultivation of the art of poetry. Their life was a hard and unremitting struggle for existence, and the rough poetry in which their inheritance of mythical lore became embodied was fitted to the rugged life they were forced to lead. Then Christianity found its way among them, and the chance was missed. The vitality of the old faith waned. Thor and Odin and Balder were dethroned by the new god from the South. Deities and heroes faded into the mists of the past, lingering, indeed, in the popular consciousness for many centuries, but growing ever more impotent to inspire poet or sage.

Yet such a body of myth and hero-story as this could never be quite lost or become wholly meaningless to the race which gave it birth, and the elementary traits of whose character were bound up within it. So it was natural that when, in modern times, and in common with the other nations of Europe, the people of the North were impelled to the development of a studied literature, they should draw largely upon the varied store of tradition for their material, and seek at a later day to do something of the work so long left undone. Thus Tegnèr in Sweden, Ewald and Oehlenschlæger in Denmark, and Björnson in Norway have found many of their themes in the treasure-house of myth and saga. Of all this modern work that of Björnson seems the most removed from modern ways of thought and expression, exhibits most clearly the modes of feeling of that quasi-historical past which it reproduces, is the most vigorous and the most elemental.

The work here translated has a definite historical basis. During the first half of the twelfth century Norway was plunged into civil strife by the pretensions to the throne of one Sigurd, surnamed " Slembe " (an adjective meaning ill-disposed or worthless), on account of his lawless youth. This Sigurd was a natural son of

the great king Magnus Barfod, and, according to the law
of Norway, the succession could not rightfully be with-
held from him on the score of his illegitimacy. The
trilogy of "Sigurd Slembe" deals with the life of this
pretender from the time when, in early manhood, he
learns the secret of his birth, to the eve of the final
struggle which crowns his life with failure and restores
peace to his long-suffering country. It is a tale of in-
domitable but ever-thwarted will, deeply tragic in its import, but not without that final touch of what the Ger-
mans call Versöhnung, and we, for want of a better
word, call reconciliation, which is the attribute of the
noblest tragic productions, and by virtue of which tragedy
fulfills its purpose as defined by Aristotle, purging the
mind of pity and fear. The consummation of a tragic
action is found in that supreme moment when the pro-
tagonist surrenders, in Schopenhauer's phrase, not merely
life, but the very desire to live. Perhaps the most perfect illustration of this in literature is the cry of Gret-
chen at the close of the first part of "Faust" — "Hein-
rich, mir graut's vor dir!" In the present work this
tragic consummation follows, in the closing act, upon the
flight of Sigurd's last remaining hope of victory. Failure, absolute and unrelieved, confronts him as the result
of all his toil. He attempts in thought each avenue of
escape, but they are all closed upon him. He has raised
his last force, and no stratagem can avail him further.
As all the events of life crowd upon the memory of a
dying man, so all Sigurd's past comes before him now
face to face with the ruin of the edifice so nearly reared
by him. And the peace of mind which he has sought
for so many years comes to him also, and all the tem-
pests of life are stilled. He sees that this was indeed

the inevitable end, and, recognizing the fitness with which events have shaped themselves, he sees life in its true aspect. No longer veiled in the mists that have hidden it from his passionate gaze, he takes note of what it really is, and casts it from him. In this hour of passionless contemplation such a renunciation is not a thing torn from the reluctant soul, but the clear solution, so long sought, of the problem so long blindly attempted.

Other scenes of great power and beauty are not lacking in this work. In the first part, Sigurd's outburst upon learning his parentage, and his departure with the crusaders; in the second part, the love scene and the parting of Sigurd and Audhild, and the sublime self-sacrifice of Earl Harald; in the third part, the king's death at Bergen, and the scene with the skald, who has traced Sigurd to his retreat in the wilds of Finland, — these are all of a nature to hold the interest spellbound. The character of Earl Harald, in the second division of the trilogy, irresistibly suggests that of Hamlet, not because the author has imitated Shakspere, but because he has conceived his melancholy Norwegian in the Shaksperean spirit. The scenes between Sigurd and Audhild have power to move the reader, by their union of simplicity with intensity of passion, almost as deeply as the love scenes of "Faust." Björnson has the power, rare even with the greater dramatists, to condense so much of passion in a single pregnant sentence, by means of a word or single phrase so to illuminate as by a lightning flash some tragic situation, as to put the ordinary rhetorical effusion of feeling to shame. He has the instinct which sees, at the fateful moment of the action, how incomparably greater and truer is a direct, rightly chosen word, than the most elaborate rhetorical amplification.

From what has been said, it will be seen that this work claims consideration chiefly as a piece of literature, irrespective of its fitness for production upon the stage. It has, however, been performed with great success, both in Christiania and Copenhagen, under the supervision of the author. The performance requires two evenings. An English audience, probably, could not be persuaded to approve of a play too long for a single performance, and the present translation is not made with any reference to the stage. The text used has been that of the fourth edition, Copenhagen, 1884.

CHICAGO, *September*, 1888.

PART FIRST.

SIGURD'S FIRST FLIGHT.

CHARACTERS.

KOLL SÆBJÖRNSON, *chieftain.*
TORA, *daughter of Sakse Vik.*
SIGURD, *her son.*

The scene is laid in the church at Stavanger, in the year 1122.

SCENE FIRST.

A small family chapel in Stavanger church, dedicated to St. Olaf.
A short bench at the left. At its side, a grated door, which forms the
sole entrance.

SIGURD.

Enters, casts his cap on the floor, and kneels before the altar.

Now shalt thou hear, St. Olaf !
To-day I conquered Bejntejn.   Bejntejn was
The strongest in the land, but now am I !
Now may I all the way from Lindesnæs
Up to the snows of Bjarm'land go, nor need
Uncover to the best, or step aside.
And where I am shall none have leave to quarrel,
To meet in strife, to threaten, or to slay.
Peace shall be everywhere, and who is wronged
He shall be righted, and the laws have sway.
And if some strong man have oppressed a weak one,
The weak shall be avenged upon the strong.
Now may I at the Thing in council sit, .
Now may I to the table of the king
Go up, sit by his side, say: here am I.
   And for all this, I thank myself alone!
Thou, Olaf, hast not helped me in the least.
I bade thee tell me who my father was,
But thou wast silent, true log that thou art.
And yet I must know ; all that I may do

Will not avail me, with my race unknown;
For when I pass, men cry: "'T is Sigurd Slembe:"
"Slembe," they say.   In vain I strike them down,
For others come who still with scornful finger
Point: "Slembe, Slembe," say they.   Oh, the shame!
I join the young men in their sports, and strike
The mightiest stroke, make the best throw, but they,
They cry not "Sigurd, hail!" nor cheer, ah no,
But rather shout, "What dost thou here, thou Slembe?"
I think at such times 't is the work of Olaf
Who yonder in the church so silent stands.
If thou shouldst will it, would my mother speak,
For surely she must know.   Oh, help me, Olaf!
Dost thou not see that I without a name
Am but a St. John's fire, alone enkindled
Deep in the vale, less seen of men than is
The least light on the heights?   Oh, set me there!
    Others have fame, and I alone have none!
I see about me men of wide renown
Who with the king went to Jerusalem.
And others still who came from Micklegarth
Laden with store of gold, and memories
So rich, their splendor haunts my very dreams.
Men journey now in hosts from England, France,
From Burgundy, and Apulia, on crusade.
Baldwin himself was but an unknown knight
And after in Jerusalem was king!
And Bohemond and Raymond, Ademar
And Tancred, Robert, all these won renown!
Give me but name and ships, that I may sail,
And I will win a kingdom for myself.
    My mother comes, — 't was here that we should meet
Before thy face, — and Koll comes too as witness.

Now if thou wilt but move her heart and tongue,
I vow that I will give to thee this cup,
This heirloom come to me from Sakse Vik.   [*He rises.*

SCENE SECOND.

SIGURD. TORA, *followed by* KOLL SÆBJÖRNSON. *They enter and kneel before the altar.*

TORA.

There is uproar without ; I hear that thou
Hast fought with Bejntejn.

SIGURD.

Ay, and conquered him.

KOLL.

Unwise it is to battle with the strongest.

SIGURD.

With whom else, then ?

KOLL.

A son of Adalbrekt
May not at all times conquer.

TORA.

Thou hast come
To bear, instead of songs of praise, a nickname.

SIGURD.

Reveal my father's name, the songs will follow.

TORA.

'T was Adalbrekt.

SIGURD.

Nay, I believe it not.
For once thou saidst in anger, 't was another.

TORA.

In anger, yes.

SIGURD.

In anger men speak truth.

TORA.

Then flies the best, and devils take its place.

SIGURD.

But they reveal the soul within.

TORA.

Away !

SIGURD.

As thou didst give me life within thy womb,
I do conjure thee that thou give me now
Birthplace and name !

TORA.

Thou shalt win both of these
After a few years' honorable strife.

SIGURD.

Shall then my best years go to build the ship,
When men no older than myself are now
Far in the south, upon the coasts of Greece ?

Thou, Koll, art witness, and as thou didst build
This church and chapel where we now are met,
I do conjure thee that thou teach my mother
What both the church and I alike demand.

KOLL.

Thou knowest, Tora, he may now compel thee,
For he is full-grown.

TORA.

Ah! but do not ask it,
For that thou askest is but thy destruction.

SIGURD.

Little I reck, so there be no disgrace.

TORA.

Disgrace there is.

SIGURD [*somewhat surprised*].

I cannot be low-born,
That I am sure, and thou art Sakse's daughter.

TORA.

And yet disgrace may come with no low birth.

SIGURD.

Yes, for the moment. But in twenty years
Shame may be buried deep as in the grave.

TORA.

And by the grave there is a fount of tears

That breaks perforce afresh, the grave reopened,
And brings me back the sorrow of the past.

SIGURD.

But many days are yet to come for me,
And heavy must they be without my father.
                              [*Koll seats himself on the bench*

TORA [*after a moment's thought*].

He lives no more !

SIGURD.

                Ah ! but his memory lives,
His might, perchance, — I ask for nothing more.
Dost thou not see how like my daily life
Is to a dog's, who, having lost his master,
Must stand perforce apart when food is dealt ?

TORA.

What matter, when thou knowest thou art the best.

SIGURD.

It may be so, but 't is a heavy life.
None will caress him, he is driven off
When he would gambol with some peasant child,
And every cur is set against his peace.
And so his eye grows wild, he learns mistrust
Of all things, and dejected slinks away.

TORA.

Oh, never, for thou courage hast and fortune;
Wilt thou but wait, thou mayst attain the highest.

SIGURD.

But wait I cannot.   Now the time is come,
We stand in Olaf's church, here is his image,
Here is a witness, and I too am here.

TORA.

Dost think a word of mine can give so much?

SIGURD.

Yes; race is power, e'en were one else alone.

TORA.

But if the race thou get'st should know us not,
Nor thee nor me? If it should cast us out?
And if it shamed me, Sigurd, unto death?

SIGURD.

My race should know me not? . . .
   [*With emphasis.*]   Then 't is because
They would withhold from me my heritage!

TORA.

Ah, do not storm so!   Hear my earnest prayer,
And tear not in thy eager thirst for fame
Thy mother's bleeding heart. Oh, pity me!
And let me keep the secret of my shame;
Let me withhold thee from thine own destruction!

SIGURD.

It is too late, for now I know at once
Too little and too much.

TORA.

Sigurd, forbear.
A moment's weakness brought upon me shame,
My life and all I had have made atonement.
One moment has revealed to thee my sin,
Thou set'st thy life at stake to know the rest.

KOLL.

It is enough.　Thou must believe thy mother.

SIGURD.

Farewell!

TORA [*anxiously*].
But whither goest thou?

SIGURD.

To sea!

TORA.

Oh, Sigurd, Sigurd!

SIGURD.

Yes, the life thou gav'st me
May be no longer by thy silence chained.
If to know all shall be to me destruction,
It is no less so that I know but this.

KOLL.

His speech betrays defiance and despair.

TORA.

Thou hast indeed his mind who made of me,
Once innocent, one of the silent folk.

My father cast me forth from out his house
With thee, new-born.   Up in the window stood
My sister, cast our garments after us
With outcry loud — and after died of sorrow.
For thou shalt know now, — thou wert born in incest !
Thy father, Sigurd, was my sister's husband,
Was King of Norway, — he was Magnus Barfod !

KOLL [*rises*].

The king !

TORA.

Yes.

SIGURD [*before the image of St. Olaf, with deep expression*].
Then we two are of one race !

KOLL.

This news is pregnant with thy destiny.

SIGURD.

Yes, it is more, far more, than I had thought.
But once conceived it opens all the world.

TORA.

But thou must keep it secret from the world.

SIGURD [*looks around*].
Yes, so it is.   Now am I free to go.

TORA.

But whither goest thou ?

SIGURD.

To the king, my brother:
He shall bestow upon me half the kingdom.

TORA.

What dost thou think of?

KOLL.

Hast thou lost thy senses?

SIGURD.

The king is bastard born, his brother too,
Who shared the kingdom with him, was a bastard.
And many kings besides, for Olaf's law
Makes no distinction.   I too have the right
To be a king!

KOLL.

But, softly, softly, friend.

SIGURD.

The royal heritage shall be shared alike.

KOLL.

He who has power shares but unwillingly.

SIGURD.

He shared with Öjstejn, and with Olaf too.

KOLL.

But he is old now, and he has a son.

SIGURD.

Yet my clear right he may deny me not.

KOLL.

It must be proved.

SIGURD.

Mother shall bear me witness.

TORA.

The ordeal will proclaim my own disgrace !

SIGURD.

When I am king, it shall be held as honor !

TORA.

For me ? Oh, never !

SIGURD.

Hear me and be calm.
For every tear in sorrow thou hast wept
Joy in thy son shall be full recompense.
Thou shalt go foremost in the great procession,
And sit upon my right hand in the hall.
Thou shalt be robed with purple and with gems.
Thou wilt bear witness ?

KOLL.

On the king it all
Depends, even at the best, and if he wills
The ordeal can but come to evil issue.

TORA.

Then were the new shame greater than the old.

SIGURD.

A rascal king ?

KOLL.

No, but a wise one, merely.
Unlikely that he heed a boy, who comes
Without a following and devoid of witness.

SIGURD.

Without a following ? But thou, Koll, art such ;
Thou art a chieftain, and of mighty race,
Thy friends are of the first men in the land.

KOLL.

He who doth follow thee on such an errand
Has broken with the king, and stakes his life.

SIGURD.

But I will make it up to thee, and more.
Thou shalt become the second in the land,
Thy race be held in such regard as mine.

KOLL.

A dangerous project, should it *not* succeed, --
A far more dangerous one, *should* it succeed.

SIGURD.

But often hast thou wished another king !

KOLL.

True.   Yet not such another one as thou.

SIGURD.

But what stands in the way ?   Wherefore not I ?
For in my birth 't was so ordained of God.

Art thou a chieftain and wilt dare refuse me
The help I crave ? Thou, who in Olaf's presence
Wast first to hear it, thou art of him chosen
To give his seed thy strength and thy protection.

KOLL.

That I may shield my country am I chosen,
And were it for her welfare, I should aid thee.
I think 't is not.

SIGURD.

Now hear me, blessed Olaf !
They will deny my right. King Jorsalfarer
Would now withhold from me that which is mine
Through God and thee. They tread upon thy law,
And God's. The law which gives me justice
Now in this place so dearly bought with tears
Wrung from a mother's eyes, with life-long sorrow,
Is torn asunder as 't were forged and void.
Be thy strength with me now and give me counsel
Whose wisdom o'er this dangerous hour shall tide
        me !
My prayer is answered ! To the king I go,
To tell him that I am his younger brother,
And that I crave not of him land, but men
And war-ships, and I will at once set forth
And seek adventures in some distant land,
Like Olaf Trygveson, like Olaf Digre,
Like Harald Sigurdson, like the king himself !

KOLL.

Be warned, nor venture near the bear's retreat ;
Nor dare to seize the prey which is his own !

SIGURD.

But I renounce my claim to share the kingdom.

KOLL.

He will not place within a rival's power
His trusty warriors.

SIGURD.

     Good; then will I seek
Without his help to gather men about me.
Many there are who long for new adventures.
He cows the great, and plunged in evil life
Rests on his old renown, and glory won
In bringing home a fragment of the cross.
But I will fire the ears of men with tales
Of other days, and deeds of old-time heroes :
Tell how their fathers' graves in distant lands
Have been ungarlanded for many years ;
Tell them of jousts on horseback and with spears
Fought in the fields of Provence, with display
Of golden armor, splendid in array.
And I will lead them where is wealth untold,
In pagan cities full of Moorish gold ;
And thence in arms into our Saviour's land,
To wash us clean of blood by Jordan's strand ;
For now within its depths the world is shaken,
The powers long crushed to earth from sleep awaken,
The peoples rise in might.   And now the soul
Of Christendom is stirred from pole to pole.
So thither shall we go as on the chase
Some storm that takes the world to its embrace,
And home returning shall such treasures bring,
.As to make dim the splendors round the king ;

Nor ears shall lack, when at the feasting-hour
Some word be said of sharing kingly power,
And if he will not, to the sword we'll fall,
And he who conquers then shall win it all.

KOLL.

Thou art forgetful of the name of this :
Here in the North we call it civil war.

TORA.

Since when the sun grew dark at Stiklestad,
A memory lingering in the Northland still,
Hath none conceived such thoughts of Cain as these.

SIGURD.

O Christ ! Not merely every port of refuge
Is closed against me, but sealed fast with sin.

KOLL.

To me it seems too wildly dost thou chase
From one side of the forest to the other.
There are so many ways —

SIGURD.

Still, still !

TORA.

My son !

Remain in peace and seek but —

SIGURD.

Never, never !
For now the earth I tread on burns beneath me !

Shall I at mine own table be a beggar?
Shall I there serve where I of right should reign?
Shall I then hold the stirrup for my brother
And stay behind, while he upon the chase
Sets forth, and but receive the filth in parting
Cast from his horse's hoofs?   Accursed thoughts!
Now like the cloud of dust about his head
In wild confusion do they mount upon me!

TORA.

But, Sigurd!

SIGURD.

With what a boyish joy I came this hour
From conflict, then just conscious of my strength!
And now my strength is as a sword whose aim
Is lofty set, that strikes and springs back shattered.
My courage and my longings knew no bound,   ·
And all the world was my inheritance.
Then got I right to claim a part thereof,
And got it but to lose it, and to lose
All faith in justice, all belief in good.
O mother, mother! thou should'st not have told me.
                              [*Casts himself on his face to earth.*

TORA.

Thou knowest now what sufferings have been mine.
                              [*Throws herself upon him.*

CHORUS OF CRUSADERS [*within the church*].

Fair is the earth,
Fair is God's heaven,
Fair is the pilgrim-path of the soul.
Singing we go

Through the fair realms of earth,
Seeking the way to our heavenly goal.

Races shall come
And shall pass away,
And the world from age to age shall roll,
But the heavenly tones
Of our pilgrim song
Shall echo still in the joyous soul.

First heard of shepherds
By angels sung,
Wide it has spread since that glad morn:
Peace upon earth!
Rejoice, all men!
For unto us is a Saviour born!

KOLL [*as the song begins*].

The song of the crusaders!

*The two others rise, Tora erect and Sigurd to his knee. Little
by little he feels himself moved, and, ere the song is ended,
has arisen, and with its close cries out.*

SIGURD.

I will take
The cross and follow!   To Jerusalem!
The path that Tancred and that Robert took
To the Lord's honor and their own renown!

TORA.

Then shall I be alone!

SIGURD.
But when men ask thee:

Where is thy son? Thou shalt say: Palestine!
Over the night's gloom streams in dawning skies
The splendor of the cross in laurel wreathed,
And he who bears the one shall win the other.

TORA.

But ere thou hast returned, I shall be dead.

SIGURD. .

But when I come, it shall be as a chieftain
Great as the king, or if I come not, still
Without me shall my fame come sorrow-clad.

TORA.

But I? Thou hast no longer thought for me!

SIGURD.

Yes, mother, — but what better canst thou wish?
Thy son's fame shall be thine. " See, Sigurd's mother!"
Thus shall men speak: "he is become a chieftain
In Palestine, a chieftain of the cross.
How proud she must be of him." Here at home
It would go ill with me. But 't is to fly
From evil thoughts to journey, thoughts of strife
At home, for, mother, deep I feel within me,
I could not bear injustice. Stay me not!
                    [*Organ and trumpets heard in the church.*
Under the cross! The cross that turns to stone
All evil spirits, and that casts out devils,
That gives the heathen stronghold to the flames!
The destroying angel now to earth descended
Chases men through the world with naked sword,
Now all the South is lit with lurid fire,

Thither I must begone! And in the battle,
Foreshadowing the last judgment, shall the soul
Be lighted up as by a lightning flash,
And then shall songs of resurrection heard
In Eastern lands bedew it with their grace.

    Listen, the mass streams from within the church,
And now the host is raised before the altar,
E'en now are sacred crosses by the priests
Dealt out. Yes, I will haste and take one too!   [*Goes.*

SCENE THIRD.

KOLL, TORA.

*The mother at first will follow her son, then turns back, falls on her
knees before St. Olaf, stretches her hands up to him, then bows down.*

KOLL.

Strive to be strong! The inevitable must
Be borne by all, as each must bear his name,
As all must bear the certainty of death.
And, Tora, what has come might not be stayed.
The wolf must rove, the eagle soar aloft,
A mighty longing is a mighty force,
And must have vent. Then, Tora, do not weep
That thou hast given birth to such a son.
The largest ship in the crusaders' fleet,
By me outfitted; it shall be his own,
And thus are wings provided for his flight,
And they will grow with years. Nay, do not thank
     me!
I owe it to a son of Magnus Barfod, —
A welcome sight to me 't is that he leaves us.
                [*The music of the organ ceases.*

TORA [*who has risen*].

That I should come to suffer this at last !
His childhood was so fair,
Boundless his love of knowledge, and his strength
Victorious ever, and his thought all joyous.
Then was I glad to think he should not bear
His father's name.   How other has it happened !
To-day with thy help has he been the victor ;
And I to-day have lost my son forever.

KOLL.

But if abroad his soul find peace again
Then hast thou won him back for more than life.

TORA.

But he with careless hand now casts away
His mother's love, and all that he is sure of ;
He spurns it all, dazzled by glittering hope.
He has no longer ears to hear our counsels,
Nor eyes to see that which is close about him ;
With yearnings so immense and will so weak,
As from a mountain he will fall at last.

KOLL.

The church is emptied, we must seek him out.   [*Goes.*

SCENE FOURTH.

TORA *will follow him, but once more turns to St. Olaf, for a moment
kneels in prayer, then quickly rises.*

TORA.

No, this time Olaf has no comfort for me,
My heart throbs now as once upon that day

When Magnus went, and I was left alone.
Where'er I turned, 't was with me as with him
Who breasts a storm, at cost of breath and strength.
The church itself seemed gloomy as the grave;
There stood the saints and over them the cross,
And none might tell me wherein I had sinned.
Why should that day be come to me again,
Again that darkness? Why now is it with me
As if I heard the cry of shipwrecked men?

    A mother suffers from the day she is one.
She loves the child before its time of birth,
Midst pangs as sharp as death she gives it life,
And for its childhood's sake she gives her health.
She is for it the eye, the foot, the arm,
The wings that lift it up into the light.

    But has she reared it, how is she repaid!
It tears itself from all her tears away,
Nor backward looks, but joyous pushes on
Until it wounded falls to earth again,
Or else gives wounds to others, but is sure,
Whiche'er of these it do, to wound its mother.

    So she gives birth, so rears unto herself
A sorrow lasting as her life is long.   *[Goes.*

SCENE FIFTH.

A cliff by the seashore. In the bay are seen the ships of the crusaders, all ready to hoist sail.

SIGURD.

Yon mighty ship that rides the wave is mine!
The first that I in all the world have owned!
Soon shall it plough its way through foaming billows,

And bear me towards my future ; at the helm
I will take heed of currents and of skies,
The high-pitched song of hope shall fill my ears,
And I at last shall taste of life indeed.

　　How great and fateful was this day to me !
I won, I lost, I won again, — and now
Take leave of country and inheritance,
And know no more than knows the wayward bird
That northward wings his flight, what life awaits me.
But thus 't is best, for in hope's wonderland
Filled with unseen adventure — there alone
May I forget all that I here have lost.

　　Even as a tree, the tallest in the forest,
Hewn to be fashioned for a mast, my life
Is torn from where it grew in vigorous health
And set at mercy of the wind and wave.

　　But may not thoughts of home have power to tempt
　　　me,
May memories sad and dear not turn me back ?
No, not if all go well,　But if, perchance,
I should, my ship and aims all crushed together,
Cling to the wreck, and God look silent on, —
O Christ be with me !　Evil thoughts swarm thick
As sharks in Southern seas about a shipwreck !

　　It cannot be that I shall fare so ill !
My calling is too high, it cannot go
Thus unrewarded — and the cross waves o'er me
Its holy banner !

SCENE SIXTH.

SIGURD, TORA.

TORA.

Art thou there, my son?

SIGURD.

Yes, here upon this rock I stood but now
And watched the ships sail by, and watched mine
    own
That yonder lies at anchor in the bay.
See, there it is! So towers some ice-clad peak
Above the forest. How the sail now swells,
How like youth's courage stands the mast erect,
See yon proud curves defiant of the storm,
And see yon deck clean as a maiden's honor
Who holds her lover to her faithful breast,
And spurns the tempters who would take his place.

TORA.

There goes a shudder through me when I think
That one should trust his fortunes to a ship.

SIGURD.

It cannot be it shall fare ill with me!
For I have well considered, and I feel
Of cheer as certain as is fortune's self.
See how the morning round about us gleams,
How shine its colors clear on my departure,
And give me promise of a glorious day.
The spring's young shoots now fill the air with fra-
    grance;

How fresh now is the breeze, how high the heavens;
Nor have I ever known, methinks, a day
My gaze could pierce so far out o'er the sea.
The all-pervading air that gently fans
Me on the cheek, doth it not bring me cheer
From heaven, from sea, from morning, and from spring?
Hail to thy journey, Sigurd Magnusson!

TORA.

This ring was placed upon my arm by Magnus
That very night when he took leave of me.
Whene'er I see it, I recall thy father,

[*Gives it to him.*

Whene 'er thou seest it, think upon thy mother,
What she has suffered for thee, how she yearns, —
Oh, take me to thee, if it shall go well!

SIGURD.

Mother, I will!

TORA.

And if it should go ill,
Then do not shun me; but come back to me!

SIGURD [*kisses her*].

May God be with thee, my beloved mother!

[*Puts the ring on.*

TORA [*turning away*].

And now in God's name on thy way set forth!

[*Bursts into tears.*

SIGURD.

Weep not, my mother, Olaf stands beside me!

[*The song of the crusaders is heard afar.*

TORA [*throws herself upon his neck*].

Come back to me, should it go ill with thee !

SIGURD.

Weep not, my mother, if we think aright
'T is a fair thing, that I may thus set forth.

TORA.

I have no word to say against it more.
But, —   [*Weeps.*

SIGURD.

Sit upon this rock, where late I sat,
And for the first time see me on my ship !

TORA.

O God !

SIGURD.

Be comforted, and I will try
To come again.   We do not leave at once.
[*Helps her upon the rock.*
See, thou art seated now where I was seated,
And soon shall be fulfilled my youthful longings.
[*Rises and kisses her.*
Farewell !   Farewell !   I will come back once more !
[*Goes.*

TORA [*on the rock*].

Sigurd ! Sigurd !
[*While the curtain falls the song is heard again.*

PART SECOND.

SIGURD'S SECOND FLIGHT.

CHARACTERS.

HARALD, *Earl of Caithness.* (*Earl also of a portion of the Orkneys, but cast out from them by his co-regent and half-brother Paul.*)

HELGA, *his mother.*

FRAKARK, *her sister.*

AUDHILD, *their niece.*

SVEN ASLEJVSSON, *a boy.*

SVEN BRIOSTREJP, *known as* SVEN VIKING.

SIGURD *of Norway.*

KÅRE, *follower of Harald.*

Other followers of Harald.

Caithness in Scotland, and Orfjara in the Orkneys. 1127.

ACT FIRST.

Caithness. A lofty, dimly-lighted hall of early twelfth century architecture.

SCENE FIRST.

FRAKARK, HELGA.

Frakark is sewing upon a red shirt, richly embroidered with gold and precious stones. Helga is at work upon a cap.

FRAKARK.

Listen to those mighty gusts! I believe we shall never have fair weather here again.

HELGA.

It is already late in the autumn.

FRAKARK.

How the house creaks!

HELGA.

It takes a heavy storm to overturn a well-built house.

FRAKARK.

The setting-in of autumn is a serious matter, especially to those whose future is uncertain.

HELGA.

Sven Viking comes to-day from the Orkneys.

FRAKARK.

What news will he bring, thinkest thou?

HELGA.

None that is good.

FRAKARK.

No. [*She leans forward on the table.*] Then we must remain snowed in here for another winter.

HELGA.

It is just three years to-day, since we were cast forth.

FRAKARK.

I could not endure it for three years longer.

HELGA.

And yet we must. There is none who can help us.

FRAKARK.

The vikings come daily home from their summer cruises. Something might be done with so many brave men.

HELGA.

But they have no leader.

FRAKARK.

I must tell thee: in the last few days I have thought of one. [*The sisters look at one another.*] What dost thou require of a leader?

HELGA.

High birth.

FRAKARK.

That, I think, he has.

HELGA.

He must be a stranger.

FRAKARK.

Wherefore?

HELGA.

A too powerful leader might become a menace to us;
therefore he must be free, without kin or friends.

FRAKARK.

Such is he, and thus have I thought too.

HELGA.

Hast thou also taken thought of the means whereby
we may win him to our cause?

FRAKARK.

There is but one bond that makes men faithful; it is
that of success.

HELGA.

It might stead him better to be faithless, for Earl
Paul has more treasure than Harald.

FRAKARK.

Knowest thou of any other bond?

HELGA.

I do.   But knowest thou the man?

FRAKARK.

What thinkest thou of him who came hither two weeks since ?

HELGA.

From Scotland ?

FRAKARK.

Yes.

HELGA.

Well.

FRAKARK.

Him I mean.

HELGA.

And him have I likewise had in mind from the day when I first saw him, but I would not be the first to speak of it. [*She rises.*

FRAKARK [*rises also*].

What hast thou thought of him, Helga ?

HELGA.

No man before him has so awed me.

FRAKARK.

And I in these two weeks have come to trust him more than Sven Viking, whom I have known from child-hood.

HELGA.

Dost thou, too, think him of high birth ?

FRAKARK.

Yes; he gives all others their due.

HELGA.

And never shares in their sports.

FRAKARK.

Why does he not tell us who he is ?

HELGA.

He waits for us to ask him.

FRAKARK.

Well, we will ask him, then, — and win him; but by what means ?

HELGA.

Let not impatience carry thee away.

FRAKARK.

But in truth, we have waited long.

HELGA.

Let us take counsel with the earl.

FRAKARK.

Thy son ?

HELGA.

Yes.

FRAKARK.

If he were but capable of counsel.

HELGA.

He is our chief; and then, he may not wish it.

FRAKARK.

Has ever any one been able to find out what he wishes?

HELGA.

Thou speakest truly; but we must consult him, after all — otherwise we might have cause for regret.

SCENE SECOND.

The same.   An old servant.

THE SERVANT.

Your niece Audhild is still away.

FRAKARK.

What dost thou mean?   Away?

THE SERVANT.

She went out yesterday, and now a day has past.   In spite of the storm she came not home.   Her maids could tell nothing, but sought for her; then old Kare went forth with many men, but she has not yet been found.

FRAKARK.

Out in such weather, alone, all the while alone!

HELGA.

. More than a whole day!

FRAKARK.

We have no neighbors here; she must be in the woods or upon the shore —

HELGA.

Or dead!

FRAKARK.

What sayest thou!

HELGA.

Hast thou searched everywhere, in every cave, every grove, every remotest nook?

THE SERVANT.

They shouted with the wind, and so must have been heard. But she came not.

FRAKARK.

I always thought that would be the end of it. She would never stay where others were, and she took no counsel.

HELGA.

All the men about the place must go forth! We too will go! Such search must be made that no spot in the great forest be overlooked.

FRAKARK.

Call out the men who are at work in the ship-houses.

THE SERVANT.

But here comes a boat.

FRAKARK.

Surely Sven Viking !

THE SERVANT.

It seems so, and he needs help in such weather.

HELGA.

He must help himself.   Come, Frakark, let us dress for the search.

FRAKARK.

But here she is already.

HELGA.

Audhild !

SCENE THIRD.

The same. AUDHILD.

FRAKARK *and* HELGA.

Where hast thou been ?

AUDHILD.

Out.

HELGA.

Thou hast put us in the greatest fright !   Thy weeping maids seek thee in the woods ; old Kåre and many men also make search for thee.   We have just heard of it all, and have been terribly alarmed —

FRAKARK.

And all on account of thy foolish caprices.

HELGA [*to the servant*].

Thou mayest go. [*He goes.*] Where hast thou been, child?

AUDHILD.

In many places.

FRAKARK.

Where didst thou sleep last night?

AUDHILD.

I did not sleep.

FRAKARK.

Thy conduct is most unseemly. Thou must obey those who have charge of thee, even if thou dost not love them. Whither art thou going?

AUDHILD.

To eat.

HELGA.

Poor child. Didst thou have nothing with thee?

AUDHILD.

No.

FRAKARK.

And now thou wilt get only cold food when thou art in need of warm. The whole place cannot be ordered after thy whims. Perhaps thou hast in mind to seek some other?

AUDHILD [*with a sigh*].

No.

FRAKARK.

And how dost thou spend thy time, my child! At thy age, there should be no need thus to reproach thee. And these escapades of thine! What is to prevent thee from being captured some day by the vikings who hug these shores, and carried off, or worse?

AUDHILD.

I can run away from them.

FRAKARK.

No maiden can run from men. Still less can she defend herself, if taken. [*Audhild smiles.*] Why dost thou smile?

AUDHILD.

I have a little hallowed knife, which came to me from my father; its blade bears the image of the blessed Mary.   [*She draws it from her bosom.*

HELGA [*aside to Frakark*].

She can win the stranger for us!

FRAKARK [*looking at her*].

Thou art right!

AUDHILD.

What do you want of me?

FRAKARK.

She is fair.   Dost thou ever think of marriage, Audhild ?

AUDHILD [*shakes her head*].

No —

FRAKARK.

And yet thou shouldst. — The other time ours was a
sorry failure, but it may chance better the next.

AUDHILD.

The safest thing is not to try at all.

HELGA.

There are men worthy a woman's love.

AUDHILD.

As *thou* shouldst well know.

HELGA [*wounded*].

Not I !   A good marriage is an honor to our kindred, and to them something is due.

AUDHILD.

Thou wouldst sell me again !

FRAKARK.

Why use such words ?   Helga says truly ; there are
men worthy a woman's love.   Thou art young and livest
only in thy fancies, but we speak from experience.

AUDHILD.

Yes, you have had experience.   He whom thou didst

choose, aunt Frakark, was called dastard; and he whom Helga chose was so worthy that he made of her — his mistress.

FRAKARK.

Silence, bold child !

AUDHILD.

I cannot keep silent, aunt, for it is my daily thought.

FRAKARK.

Experience includes more than what one alone has lived through : in such case its counsels were indeed often of doubtful worth.

HELGA.

Trust to us, who are here in thy mother's place, for we would not offer our child the sorrows we ourselves have borne. We speak not to thee of unwilling marriage, but ask only that thou mistrust not all men, believe not that all are unworthy. We mean no more than this.

FRAKARK.

Young people imagine that they make great discoveries about life, or else they think they are not understood, because men do not seem to notice them. But we understand thee well, Audhild. Yet I will not now tell thee what thou longest for; I will but say, thou art weary of Caithness.

AUDHILD.

Weary to death.

FRAKARK.

What wouldst thou say, were we to leave it?

AUDHILD.

I have been so often deceived, that I will not again
believe until I stand once more upon my native soil.

FRAKARK.

Thou thyself mayest perchance bring that to pass.

HELGA [*to Frakark*].

No more now.

AUDHILD.

What meanest thou?

FRAKARK.

There is a noteworthy stranger here.   Thou hast seen
him?

AUDHILD.

Yes.

HELGA [*as before*].

No further.

FRAKARK.

What thinkest thou of him?

AUDHILD.

Ha! ha! ha!   Be sure that from this time on I shall
hate him.

[*She puts her hand to her breast with an expression of pain,*

HELGA.

What is it, child ?

AUDHILD.

You should not vex me to-day.   My breast pains me ;
I am faint.

FRAKARK.

Why didst thou not say so at once, child ?

[*Audhild goes.*

SCENE FOURTH.

FRAKARK, HELGA.

FRAKARK.

She has a most passionate nature.

HELGA.

And the more it is vexed, the higher rise the waves.

FRAKARK.

I do not understand thy caution.

HELGA.

No, thou understandest nothing but thine own will,
and [*as she sits down*] for that reason things have fared
as they have.

FRAKARK.

What sayest thou ?   [*Pausing a moment.*]   I am
never sure whether thou art with or against me.

HELGA.

When violent measures are in question, I am always against thee.

FRAKARK.

But so little has been accomplished here.

HELGA.

Harald grows ever more unhappy — and so it seems that too much has been accomplished.

FRAKARK.

And yet I find thy counsel in all that has hitherto been done.

HELGA.

What will a mother not devise for her son's sake ; — and yet she may stop short of its performance.

FRAKARK.

Why dwell upon him alone! That it is that weakens thy will. I have children, too, but I think neither of them nor of myself alone : it were too narrow an ambition.

HELGA.

Yet each of them has an immortal soul.

FRAKARK.

I am far from feeling sure of the individual immortality so much preached of ; but there is an immortality of which I am sure : it is that of the race. Sow but for that, and the race itself, in its own autumn and springtime, will carry on the work; the one will harvest and the other provide for the future. Seen from all sides, life is but a struggle between different races, and the waves of battle beat most furiously about the throne. Two kings engage in strife, and races take sides with them from noble down to peasant; they who win cast forth from possessions and country them who lose, but hardly has conquest been achieved when the conquerors fight among themselves for precedence, and, chainwise, one race draws another after it, either up to the throne or down to the abyss.

HELGA.

Countries then need no laws!

FRAKARK.

No! For my part I know no other law than that of blood; no other sin than that of abstention from the strife. Link must strengthen link, that the race may become the first in its native land. And I will not rest, until your son is once more earl of all the Orkneys and of Caithness, that he may make our brother earl of Torså and provide good marriages for our daughters. Land and people all about must be ours. For thus alone am I sure of owning the grave in which I shall be laid, and sure that it will be honored by those who come after. [*She takes the shirt in her hands and goes to the door. After opening it, she exclaims.*] Sven Viking marches up to the house at the head of his men; we must go to meet him!

HELGA.

I come!   [*She follows in haste.*

SCENE FIFTH.

HARALD, SVEN ASLEJVSSON.

SVEN ASLEJVSSON [*peering in*].

Yes ; they are gone.

HARALD [*enters: they step forward*].

Say, the wolf we caught in the wolf-caves ought to be called aunt, ought it not ?

SVEN.

Yes, aunt ; it would look like her, too, if it wore a head-dress.

HARALD.

We will kill him to-day, won't we ?

SVEN.

We can do it right away ; it will give us something to do.

HARALD.

But slowly, Sven.

SVEN.

Yes, slowly.

HARALD.

Tell me, how shall we do it ?

SVEN [*seated on the floor before the earl*].

We might fasten knives to long poles and stab it.

HARALD.

Yes, yes; and then?

SVEN.

Then we can throw fire upon it.

HARALD.

Yes, yes.   How wicked thou wilt be when thou art come to power!   And then?

SVEN.

Then we can tease it with sticks armed with spikes.

HARALD.

Ho, ho, how wicked he grows!

SVEN.

Wicked?   It killed our best dog.

HARALD.

Truly, I forgot, it killed Balder.   Aunt, too — Suppose we let it loose?

SVEN.

Why?

HARALD.

Among aunt's flocks.   What sayest thou?·

SVEN.

Then it would get into thine, too.

HARALD.

True.   Well, we will kill it.

SVEN.

Come on, then!

HARALD.

But it is an ugly thing to look at: cannot some one else do it?

SVEN.

Why, dear, the fun of it is in looking on!

HARALD.

·True also, I had forgotten. But — thou mightest look on, and tell me about it afterwards.

SVEN.

That is the way thou always art!

HARALD.

No, no, little Sven, be good, and I will find some other sport for thee. What is that? The storm?

SVEN.

No, it is a shout. [*Clambers up to the window.*] It is Sven Viking with all his men. He has come at last.

HARALD.

So it is. The stranger has his place at board and bed. We shall soon have quarrels enough here, Sven.

SVEN.

Who will win?

HARALD.

Sven Viking will win. I like not the stranger, dost thou?

SVEN.

I like no one here.

HARALD.

No, let them fight, we shall be rid of them! But it
was not I who bestowed the place on him. It is thy
fault.

SVEN.

But I never leave thee.

HARALD.

No, and so they cannot harm thee. Dost thou like
Sven Viking?

SVEN.

No one! No one!

HARALD.

Nor I. Oh, for him who should dare, Sven!

SVEN.

What wouldst thou then?

HARALD.

I will not say now. But one thing I dare do, if it
last much longer.

SVEN.

What is it?

HARALD.

Die.

SVEN.

Dear earl!

HARALD [*who has sat down*].

Tell me about Sigurd Jorsalfarer.

SVEN.

Always about him!

HARALD.

He is a great chieftain, Sven.

SVEN.

He was: he is mad now.

HARALD.

What made him mad, thinkest thou?

SVEN.

A fish came to him in the bath.

HARALD [*shaking his head*].

H'm, H'm! Dost thou know what the fish is?

SVEN.

The fish?

HARALD.

It is an evil thought, that keeps one from sleep.

SVEN [*going up to him and stroking his hair*].

Think no more of it, earl! Let us do something, — let us sing!

HARALD.

Yes, little Sven, yes ; let us sing.

SVEN.

About the king without lands or queen ; the song that
thou madest.

HARALD.

Yes, that will do, yes.   Sing thou the refrain, and I
will sing the song.

SVEN.

Not so slowly.

HARALD.

No.   [*Sings.*]   Will that do ?

SVEN.

Yes, that is right.   [*Harald is silent.*]   Now, earl !

HARALD.

No, I will not.

SVEN.

What shall we do, then ?

HARALD.

We will amuse ourselves to-morrow, little Sven, to-
morrow.

SVEN.

There comes thy mother, earl.

HARALD.

So! Then an end to my peace!   [*Rises.*

SCENE SIXTH.

HARALD, HELGA, SVEN ASLEJVSSON.

HELGA.

Good morning, my son!

HARALD.

That is more than I knew before.

HELGA.

How is it with thee?

HARALD.

Not so ill as with the ambitious, nor so well as with
the dead.

HELGA [*showing the cap*].

I have made thee a pretty cap, is it not? Do me the
kindness to accept it.

HARALD [*as he takes it*].

Thanks. It will become me well on my marriage day.

HELGA.

What dost thou mean by that, my son?

HARALD.

I mean, mother, that I am deeply in love, and think
to change my estate.

HELGA.

There is nothing in the way.

HARALD.

Dost thou think it, mother? Yes, the cap is pretty;
it will look well enough upon my head in death.

HELGA.

In death?

HARALD.

A living head does not fit me. And the bride of
whom I spoke, — dost thou understand Latin, mother?

HELGA.

No.

HARALD.

If thou didst, I might tell thee her name in Latin.
But in all tongues alike she is dark and very quiet.
What hast thou bought of me with this cap?

HELGA.

It is a mother's gift.

HARALD.

Thy gifts are as those of Jacob to Pharaoh. Thou
wouldst enter into Goshen.

HELGA.

What dost thou name thus?

HARALD.

My thoughts, dear mother. Be not vexed. I will

use another figure. Every time thou givest me aught,
thou dost but sell a fragment of me to my aunt.

HELGA.

By all the saints, what sayest thou?

HARALD.

Be not vexed; thou art not the only one to see his
image in the water. Come, what is it thou wilt have of
me to-day?

HELGA.

It seems that thou art angry with me. Is it because
Sven Viking is again trying to deal with thy brother?

HARALD.

I say naught: I am never angry. Come, what wilt
thou?

HELGA.

Thou dost not treat me courteously.

HARALD.

I beg, then, for thy pardon.

HELGA.

Oh, didst thou but know, Harald!

HARALD [*giving way*].

Spare thy pathos, mother; thou knowest I am as easily
moved without it.

HELGA.

Tell me thy meaning, and we will act according to thy wish.

HARALD.

For God's sake, no ; I have no meaning.

HELGA.

But why not trust in me? I surely am worthy of it. I have suffered much for thy sake.

HARALD.

Much! Ay, "much" may be a great deal, but much from much leaves naught. Let that drop, mother. But hasten, hasten, I have other things to do; say, what wilt thou buy of me to-day?

HELGA.

Buy of thee, I? I who have given thee my whole life! Canst thou believe that I still think of self? As truly as there is a heaven above us —

HARALD.

There is a hell beneath us. Yes, yes, mother, keep thy thoughts from straying upwards. The world we dwell in is wild enough.

HELGA.

Thou shalt never succeed in wearing out my forbearance. I held thee in my arms as a child, and, looking though thy infant eyes into thy soul saw there the germs of good. It is some other than thou that now speakest to me ; but I will patiently wait till thy wild words and deeds shall give place to the old smile which made me first feel that I was indeed a mother. Oh, wouldst thou but tell me what I might do to behold it once more !

HARALD.

I will tell thee quickly : thou must go to bed, for dreams bring back many things that life knows no longer. They say, too, that a young man lying in death may once again wear the look of his childhood : so thou must wait.

HELGA.

Oh, Harald, hast thou ever thought that thou mightest kill me ?

HARALD.

Yes, dear mother. Had I not, many things would be other than they now are.

HELGA.

I love thee more than all the earth besides, and there is nothing in all the circle of the world or of thought that I would shrink from, if it might purchase thee a happy hour.

HARALD.

Yes, a mother's love may be a fearful thing.

HELGA.

My son !

HARALD.

Come, come, mother ! The suffering is so long, and

the name so short.　We bear the one, let not the other frighten thee.　Mother, thy errand!

HELGA.

Thy many words —

HARALD.

Yes, they are my fence!　Thy errand!

HELGA.

God! nothing but my errand.

HARALD.

Is it too much to ask?　You have driven me from one earldom, you have taken possession of the other, and of my power and my house and much besides. And now I beg of you but one small thing; to be left in peace.　But that, it seems, is the hardest thing of all for you will in no wise grant it me.

HELGA.

Hast thou through our fault lost the things of which thou speakest, it was, believe me, out of love for thee, — a love, perhaps, that erred.　And believe, too, that we think night and day of how we may restore them to thee.　We have just made the last effort possible, by peaceable means, and Sven Viking has just returned. Meet him with friendliness, hear the message he brings, and tell us thy will.

HARALD.

The fox chased the frightened lambs before him.　I

know thine errand.   I have sent no message to my brother, I have done naught.   I will hear naught.

HELGA.

But it is done in thy name, and for the people's sake,
for ours and thine own —

HARALD.

Well, then, yes; as you will, — yes.   But let it
quickly be over.   [*Helga remains motionless.*]   Is there
anything more?

HELGA.

If it were only I who might ask that!

HARALD.

Yet anything more?

HELGA.

No, no; there is nothing more.   [*She goes.*

SCENE SEVENTH.

HARALD, SVEN ASLEJVSSON. *Afterwards* FRAKARK,
HELGA, SVEN VIKING.

HARALD [*seats himself*].

Would they but leave me in peace!   There are too
many wolves for a single dog.   [*Sinks back.*

SVEN ASLEJVSSON [*who has seated himself upon a footstool*].

What a day for delays and vexation!

FRAKARK *enters, followed by* HELGA *and* SVEN VIKING.

FRAKARK.

We come hither with Sven, our foremost man; he brings messages from thy brother. [*Harald rises. Sven Aslejvsson goes forward and stands at his side.*] Thou thyself shalt hear, if agreement be possible.

SVEN VIKING.

God's peace with you, lord earl! I come to-day in rough weather, but I wished to deliver my message.

HARALD.

I have bargained neither for the weather nor for the message, and so I cannot say welcome. But thou shalt thyself be received as befits thee.

FRAKARK.

Care has been taken for that.

HARALD [*softly, to the boy*].

His face is overcast; he surely knows that the stranger has his place.

SVEN VIKING.

You brothers are much unlike. Paul is silent and sparing of speech, so that men call him the taciturn; but thou hast many words, more often than there is need for, and therefore they call thee the loquacious.

HARALD.

I can tell thee something yet stranger: we were once

much the same, but that which made him silent made me full of speech.

[He seats himself, takes the boy on his knee, and leans his head on the boy's shoulder.

FRAKARK.

Do thine errand, Sven, and as the earl forgets to thank thee for thy trouble, I will do it. We should not forget the rough weather in which thou hast fared forth, and left, perhaps, an earl to whom thou wert more welcome.

SVEN VIKING.

I have a word to say of that later. But first I will deliver what I have been charged with; although it seems I have little thanks for it.

SVEN ASLEJVSSON.

Yes, he knows it.

SVEN VIKING [*stepping nearer*].

Earl Paul sends you God's greeting and his own. He says to you that the half of the kingdom which you got, although not born in wedlock, from your father, you have forfeited by what since has happened. But when I announced to him your present will, he said that for the sake of the friendship he once bore you, he would yet do what he might. But he must impose a new condition.

HARALD.

You may share with me, said the wolf to the hare, but when you have eaten your portion, I will eat you.

SVEN VIKING.

The condition is, that you come back alone, with
neither aunt nor mother.   [*Silence.*

FRAKARK.

I hope thou seest the drawn sword which lies in the
message of peace?

HARALD.

Sharpen it, thou!

FRAKARK.

Dost thou understand aright?   She, who for thy sake
lived sixteen years with thy father, Earl Håkon, despite
the scorn and the hatred of his people and lawful wife;
thy mother, who loves thee, Harald, more than another
may comprehend; it is thy mother who shall be re-
jected. [*Silence.*] Thou surely canst not understand?

HARALD [*motionless*].

Yes, I understand.

FRAKARK.

Thou canst not, Harald, else wouldst thou speak to
her.   Behold her fear — lovest thou thy brother more?

HELGA.

Frakark!

HARALD [*as before*].

Ah, yes, I understand it fully: I must either slay
my brother or slay my mother.

BOTH SISTERS.

What?

HARALD.

I cannot return to the Orkneys until·my brother is slain, for should I accept the condition which he has named, I should slay my mother.

HELGA [*approaching him*].

Yes, shouldst thou leave me, it would kill me! May God ever bless thee for the words — the first words of love I have had from thee in three years. Now I see it all. [*Clasping his knees.*] Thou mayest upbraid me, for thou art ill; but I know now that thou lovest me still. O Harald, let it appear in this hour.

HARALD [*who has put the boy aside, and then arisen*].

Have I said aught that should bring thee to thy knees before me, I beg for thy forgiveness.

FRAKARK.

The flame of her maternal love sinks at thy look as before a chilling mist. Helga! Canst thou not put out the hearth-fire and go forth into the great light of the world? Beasts love their own brood alone: men should hold more within their grasp.

HARALD [*who is again seated, to the boy*].

Thou must remember what she says, when thou art grown to manhood.

FRAKARK.

To come back now from this confusion to our business. Was Torkel Fostre present when Paul delivered this message ?

SVEN VIKING.

-It came from him.

FRAKARK.

I thought it.

SVEN VIKING.

He strode forward and said : For twenty years have Helga and Frakark stirred up dissension in the Orkneys. It was they who caused the father of the earls to strive for sole power, they at whose bidding he slew Magnus, Torkel Fostre's friend. It is they, too, who have set the brothers at war, for their sole thought is of supreme power. And as long as they shall live will peace remain afar.

FRAKARK.

That saying I will turn about thus : as long as Torkel Fostre shall live, there will be no peace. Thanks for thy mission, Sven. Leave us, now, and make thyself at home.

SVEN VIKING.

That might be — did I only know whither to go.

HARALD *and* SVEN ASLEJVSSON [*to one another*].
Now it is coming !

FRAKARK.

Whither thou shalt go ?

SVEN VIKING.

Hitherto have I always had here at Caithness the first place at board and bed, but while I was absent on the earl's errand, it has been given to a stranger.

FRAKARK.

That I have seen ; but who has done so ?

HELGA [*hastily*].

Surely, it was done thoughtlessly.

SVEN VIKING.

No, they say it was done at the earl's command.

HELGA.

That cannot be ; thou must have failed to understand.

HARALD.

Has it been said that I commanded it ?

SVEN VIKING.

Your boy said so.

HARALD [*taking him by the ear*].

How canst thou say such things, boy ?

SVEN ASLEJVSSON.

Oh, lord earl, I knew no better. He who came was so tall and grand.

HARALD.

For that trick I shall pay thee as I never have before.

HELGA [*to Sven Viking*].

Thou hast heard, it was but a child's trick.

SVEN VIKING.

I have heard. A man may not fight with boys; else should Sven be Sven's bane.

HARALD [*to Sven Aslejvsson*].

Thou must remember him too, when thou art grown.

SVEN VIKING.

But he, who was so sure of himself that he took the place, must prove himself able to defend it. Even now are the people gathered in the court-yard. [*Goes.*

HARALD *and* SVEN ASLEJVSSON.

Now it will begin!

HELGA.

Nay, Sven, bethink thyself!

FRAKARK.

We, Sven, will make good thy loss.

HELGA.

Be reconciled in friendship. [*Sven has disappeared.*

SCENE EIGHTH.

The same without Sven Viking. AUDHILD *enters.*

HELGA.

This does not augur well.

FRAKARK.

Why does he not turn the boy away?

SVEN ASLEJVSSON.

I must get up in the window to see. [*Climbs up.*]
Just so — they are in the court-yard, all the men are
coming out, Sven is speaking. See there! The others
go to one side. Come, earl, it is going on finely.

HARALD [*steps to the window and then back again*].

No, I do not want to look. Tell me about it.
[*Audhild and Helga are upon either side of him, and endeavor
to peer out.*]

FRAKARK.

It might have been avoided. [*She goes to the window.*] Sven has thrown off his cloak already.

SVEN ASLEJVSSON.

The stranger smiles: he is not afraid.

HARALD.

Have they drawn their swords?

SVEN ASLEJVSSON.

No, not yet. They are still speaking — now Sven —
now the other. See there! The stranger sprang upon
him! Ha!

ALL.

They fall!

SVEN ASLEJVSSON.

The stranger underneath!

ALL.

Oh, no!

HARALD.

How is it? How is it?

SVEN ASLEJVSSON.

I have never seen its match! [*Jumps down.*] The
stranger sprang upon him like a cat, threw himself down
with Sven, himself underneath, and then, with legs and
hands to Sven's breast, threw him off, several feet away
—then sprang up, drew his sword, and laid it upon
him.   [*Cries without.*

FRAKARK [*coming forward*].

I have never seen the like.

HELGA [*further back*].

He will serve our purpose.

FRAKARK.

If he conquer Sven Viking, none can withstand him.
                                          [*Cries without.*

HELGA.

Hear, how they hail him!

FRAKARK.

Audhild, go out and call him in.

AUDHILD.

I?

HELGA.

She means, you shall ask one of the men to do it.

[*Audhild goes, the cries are renewed.*

FRAKARK.

Hear me! That man is born to be a leader. We will now send Earl Paul his answer.

HARALD.

That he is made for, surely. I have felt all along that I could not bear him. Sven, bring the chess-board. We will play the game in which the chieftain stands still, and the woman has all the power.

[*Seats himself, Sven goes, and returns with the chessmen.*

SCENE NINTH.

The same. AUDHILD, *after her* SIGURD, *in knight's costume of Scotch cut.*

SIGURD.

God's peace in this house!

FRAKARK.

We have all beheld thy deed, and now bid thee approach.

SIGURD.

He would seize upon the place that you had honored me with.   [*Harald and Sven sit down at the right and play.*

HELGA.

Thou hast come from our friend, the Scottish king?

SIGURD.

From him last.

HELGA.

But thou art hardly Scotch ?

SIGURD.

I am a Northman.

HELGA.

How didst thou happen, then, to be in Scotland ?

SIGURD.

My ship was driven thither in a storm.   I was asked
to stay, and did so.

FRAKARK.

Whither wert thou bound, when thou camest thither ?

SIGURD.

Upon crusade.

HELGA.

And now ?

SIGURD.

If nothing else is offered me — on crusade.

FRAKARK.

Hast thou no object in view ?

SIGURD.

None.

HELGA.

Hast thou kindred ?

SIGURD.

I have a mother.

HELGA.

Thou hast a mother.

FRAKARK.

Who art thou ?

SIGURD.

What my deeds make me.

FRAKARK.

We will not question thee further. Thou hast been here for a fortnight, we have asked thee neither of thy home nor of thy mission. And what is now in question is this : if thou art as well pleased with us as we with thee, we would ask for thy service.

SIGURD.

It falls out well, for my errand had to do with that.

HELGA.

We are pleased to hear it.

SVEN ASLEJVSSON [*to the earl*].

Thou dost not attend.

HARALD.

Yes, I attend.

FRAKARK.

Speech is now made of an expedition against Paul in Orkney.

SIGURD.

I have heard it.

FRAKARK.

But the earl is sick; we have no leader.

SIGURD.

I knew that, too.

FRAKARK.

We have trust in thee; wouldst thou not consent to act as chieftain of the men thou seest here, and of many others?

SIGURD.

The men are very wild.

FRAKARK.

Thou shouldst have the earl's power over them.

HELGA.

But the earl will not have it so, I can see.

FRAKARK.

Who asks him?

HELGA.

He will not! and it shall not be!

FRAKARK.

What does this mean, and at the last moment? Harald, dost thou not wish for war?

HARALD.

Did some one ask me a question?

FRAKARK.

Thou knowest well, nothing may be gained by peace; here, now, is the opportunity to try other means.

HARALD.

One way to the gallows is as good as another, said the boy; I am willing to take the shortest. [*Goes on playing.*

FRAKARK.

Can one understand from that what he wishes?

HELGA.

If we should act awrong!

FRAKARK.

I have often said it, only in Orfjara can he be happy again. [*To Sigurd.*] Dost thou accept the offer?

SIGURD.

That depends. If all will swear to obey me, and I receive commands from none, I will be the leader.

[*The earl rises, but seats himself again.*

HELGA.

That is too much power for one man.

FRAKARK.

Then wilt thou be lord, and we but followers.

SIGURD.

Otherwise I should but follow, and you command.

FRAKARK.

Thou shalt have it as thou wilt.

HELGA.

But the earl?

FRAKARK.

Will reap only profit by it.

HARALD.

Now I am sold, little Sven; what wilt thou give for
me now?

SVEN.

I will give a whole earldom for thee now.

FRAKARK [*to Sigurd*].

The woman thou seest is our niece.

SIGURD [*greeting Audhild*].

So I have heard.   [*Audhild draws back.*

SIGURD.

Can the men pledge their obedience at once?

FRAKARK.

I am glad that we have at last found a man who will
not flag.

HELGA.

What reward do you require?

SIGURD.

When I have done the work you may give me what you will.

FRAKARK.

He is after my own heart. Audhild, see that the men are called together for council.   [*Audhild goes.*

HARALD [*rising*].

Let us go now, Sven, there are so many people coming.   [*Sven gathers up the chessmen.*

HELGA.

Dost thou leave us?

HARALD.

I may be spared, perhaps.

FRAKARK.

But the men are coming now.

HARALD [*departing*].

Say that I am sick. You will not be far from the truth.

SCENE TENTH.

The same, without Harald and Sven. AUDHILD.

HELGA.

Dost thou see? He approves it not.

FRAKARK.

We may not pause half-way. [*To Sigurd.*] The earl seems to you to act strangely?

SIGURD.

H'm; he who is not strong sinks often beneath the weight of his own thoughts.

HELGA.

Thine answer was kindly.

SIGURD.

Good fortune alone can cure such sickness.

HELGA.

Dost thou think it? If all should fare well —

SIGURD.

He would soon be himself again.

AUDHILD [*enters*].

The storm has carried the roof from off the ship-houses, and therefore many men are at work there. But word has been sent.

FRAKARK.

Thanks, my child. [*Speaks to her, and adjusts her dress.*]

HELGA [*to Sigurd*].

Thou seemest very sure that with good fortune he will be himself again.

SIGURD.

For I know something of his case. It is hard to

strive with kindred, and through the fault of kindred to lose all that one is born to is hard also. There are many who dare not choose between such conditions. But the choice once made, then comes peace of mind.

HELGA.

Thou must have known something of the sort.

SIGURD.

He who cannot help himself finds often solace in helping others.

HELGA.

And therefore art thou come ?

SIGURD.

In proof thereof I have a letter from king David of Scotland.

FRAKARK [*coming up*].

A letter from the king of Scotland ?

SIGURD [*giving it to her*].

To you.

FRAKARK.

I cannot read.   Here, Helga.

HELGA.

No, my eyesight has failed me of late.   But Audhild can read it.

FRAKARK [*to Audhild*].

Come hither and read.

AUDHILD [*reads*].

" David, king of Scotland, sends God's greeting and his own to Frakark, daughter of Maddad. Since we have learned the straits of thy nephew Harald,— to whom God grant many days, — we send thee by this token a man who can surely help you. He has been with me for three years, and for two of them has held the leadership in his own hands, and better man have I never had. He will now away, which grieves me, but it likewise gladdens me, since it is in thy cause. The strife of Earl Harald and his brother he has taken much to heart; he has heard that you need a leader, and offers himself. And my word is this, that you will find no better man. May all the saints pray Lord Jesus, our Saviour, to take us under his protection."

FRAKARK.

And thou hast not given us this before ?

SIGURD.

I wished first to learn how things stood here, and that was not to be done in a day.

FRAKARK.

Unlooked-for succor is like a guide at the crossway. We know, now, what our path must be.

HELGA [*taking Sigurd's hand*].

Thanks ! And may God reward thee, for I cannot.

SCENE ELEVENTH.

The same: the men enter.

FRAKARK.

Men of Caithness, and strangers ! You have often said
that you would join in an expedition against Earl Paul,
for you have suffered from the wrong done by him. If
your ships are in order, there is a man here who can
direct you whither to steer them. When brave men go
forth to war, no words are needed — least of all a
woman's. But after victory they are more fitting, if good
gifts go with them. As the oldest of our race I promise
you these, but ask of you that you swear obedience to
him whom we give you for a leader. [*Raising a cru-
cifix.*] In the sight of the Redeemer, pledge to him
[*pointing to Sigurd*] the obedience that men owe to
their chieftain.

THE MEN.

We pledge it to him !

· FRAKARK [*to Sigurd*]:

Now speak, who hereafter art to command them.

SIGURD.

I have never spoken at Thing or at king's council.
[*Approaching them.*] But it seemed to me there were
some who gave no pledge. Let them leave ; and this
be said to thee, Sven Viking, yonder by the door !

SVEN VIKING [*making his way forward*].

I will go with you — but as a free man, giving help

or not, as I choose. We shall see who will first show his heels, he who was so fierce, or he who was silent.

SIGURD.

Upon such self-appointed terms comes no one. But that thou mayst know that I esteem thee, Sven Viking, I offer thee the fourth part of the spoils that fall to the leader's share.

SEVERAL OF THE YOUNGER MEN.

It was a fair offer.

SEVERAL OF THE ELDERS.

Yes, it was no mean one.

TWO MEN [*to Sven*].

Thou canst accept it, Sven.

KÅRE.

Yes, there is no shame in doing it.

FRAKARK [*standing by Helga and Audhild*].

He understands them.

KÅRE [*turns toward Sigurd and removes his cap*].

There are many here who in former days followed the noble chieftain Magnus Barfod. And thou art as like to him as one drop of water is to another, and therefore we will follow thee!

ANOTHER OLD MAN.

Yes, he is like unto him who bore the lion upon the red shirt!

MANY.

He is a son of Magnus !

[*In the mean while several of the younger men have advanced,
one after another, to look at him. Sigurd has come forward
and stands near the women.*

SVEN VIKING [*forward*].

And for that came I in with the others.   For when
I heard that said by many trustworthy men, I held it no
shame to be overcome.   [*Sigurd crosses to the other side.*

HELGA [*to Frakark*].

We have done a rash deed !   He will prove a danger
to my son !

FRAKARK.

Dost thou think so, Helga ?

SIGURD [*advancing quickly towards the men*].

Strive, then, to be like his men, for no warriors had
ever nobler memory.   To-night we will drink to each
other, to-morrow man our ships !

ALL.

Yes, to-night for pleasure, to-morrow —

[*They talk together in groups.*

ACT SECOND.

A hall in Orfjara [Orkney]. It is dark.

SCENE FIRST.

Sigurd Slembe *and* Sven Viking.

Both in travel-stained costume. The latter bears a lantern, and things which betoken a journey.

SIGURD.

What a greeting is this, when we return from an expedition which has conquered the rest of the land !

SVEN VIKING [*striking a light*].

Perhaps they are not up yet.

SIGURD [*laying weapons and cloak aside*].

Not up !   The crusader priests are at morning prayers on the chapel hill ; all are up.

SVEN VIKING.

Then they have not seen us.

SIGURD.

Thou meanest not what thou sayest.

SVEN VIKING.

Neither wilt thou believe me, perhaps, when I tell thee that Torkel Fostre was slain this night.

SIGURD.

Impossible !   My honor was pledged for the prisoner's life !

SVEN VIKING.

It was too thin a wall to set between Frakark and him she hates.

SIGURD.

Then I leave at once.

SVEN VIKING.

Stay, rather !   Take possession of thy land !

SIGURD.

My land ?

SVEN VIKING.

The Orkneys are a Norse fief, and the brothers have forfeited their rights in them.

SIGURD.

Away !

SVEN VIKING.

Thou art Magnus Barfod's son.   Here art thou at home.

SIGURD.

Away !

SVEN VIKING.

All the men love thee.

SIGURD.

Then I must go.   Some one must bind my wound.

SVEN VIKING [*takes his lantern and follows*].

Hear you the uproar from the hill ?   The people have learned of Torkel Fostre's murder.   Now let it be !

[*Both go.*

SCENE SECOND.

HELGA [*enters from the right, and listens at a door on the left*].

Yes, he is up. But I saw a light at daybreak. So he sleeps no better in Orfjara. But he has won again what he lost, so, it was not that. [*Listens again.*] His boy surely sleeps, he moves so quietly. So calm within, and without such an uproar from the earliest dawn! The crusader priests urge our people to seek Christ's grave. Where they are, watchfulness is needful. But what a noise! Surely they are not now talking of crusade! And if they speak of aught else, it must be of us, of our plans. Words may fall to thwart us; we should have been there. Sigurd has returned, but may not be trusted; he wins the people more and more. In some heated moment, — Harald must go with us up to the hill! [*Listens, then knocks.*] He paused — no, he walks again. [*Knocks.*] No answer! [*Stands still for a moment.*] The noise still increases. We women cannot go up there alone, — he must go with us. [*Calls.*] Harald! Harald! it is I! [*The door is opened.*

HELGA [*starts backward*].

Saints of heaven! how pale he is!

HARALD [*softly, from within*].

They hover about me night and day, like ravens about a corpse. Come in, but quietly.

[*She enters: he closes the door.*

SCENE THIRD.

SIGURD.   AUDHILD [*with a little flask and bandages*].

AUDHILD.

Where are you wounded, say you ?

SIGURD [*holding out his right hand*].

Here, between the two fingers — a spear-prick.   Pour on a drop or two from the flask I gave you, and then bind it up.   They never succeed in dealing me deep wounds.

AUDHILD.

But you deal such full often.

SIGURD.

And even when I am wounded, it quickly heals.

AUDHILD.

It is a fortunate thing for you, who fare so far abroad.

SIGURD.

You are spilling the drops upon the floor.

AUDHILD.

I was up very early, and my hand trembles.

SIGURD.

You do not seem to be weak.

AUDHILD.

I try not to be.   Will you hold the flask ?

SIGURD [*taking it*].

This balm is a noble thing. I have it from my
mother. It came from Ireland with Magnus Barfod.

AUDHILD.

It availed him little at the last.

SIGURD.

Nothing avails at the last. [*She gazes upon him.*]
But when it has come to that pass, it is surely sweet to
give up.

AUDHILD.

It is all done.

SIGURD.

And I thank you. [*Smiling.*] I cannot offer the
right hand. [*Extends the left.*] How warm yours is !
Mine is cold.

AUDHILD.

That betokens health.

SIGURD.

So they say.   [*He looks for a place to put the flask.*

AUDHILD.

Shall I not keep it for you ?

SIGURD.

That would be of little use to me, for I must now depart.

AUDHILD.

You depart?

SIGURD.

Yes; I have finished here, and others take my work upon them.

AUDHILD.

What mean you?

SIGURD.

You do not know, then? While I was away, Torkel Fostre was slain in his prison.

AUDHILD.

Sancta Maria, Torkel slain!

SIGURD.

Yes. I had promised him freedom upon my honor, when all should be settled. The pledge is broken, but not by me.

AUDHILD.

By whom, then?

SIGURD.

That may be guessed and said. [*Silence.*] Hear the uproar from the chapel hill! They are now talking of the murder. The crusader priests journey the country round, and seize every opportunity to urge men to take the cross. The minds of the people are disturbed. When holy things stir the thoughts of men, they will not bear what they otherwise would. But they who have brought this about must abide the outcome!

AUDHILD.

Now we are indeed undone.

SIGURD.

However that may be, I must depart at once. Should I remain, the murder would appear to be mine.

AUDHILD.

None would believe it of you. And if it were believed, should you, who stand so high, fear a mere phantasm?

SIGURD.

One's memory is more than that.

AUDHILD.

But there are claims to which even judgment must give way.

SIGURD.

Here are none such.

AUDHILD.

Helga and her son.

SIGURD.

If I am to further their cause, I must not become entangled in the evil works of others.

AUDHILD.

But Earl Harald should not suffer for the deeds of the others.

SIGURD.

That is his fate. Suspicion and dishonor are round about him, and nothing can help him more. Then I would not become too closely entangled, for my sole happiness is in freedom.

AUDHILD.

I thought so too — once, but found it an illusion.

[*Silence.*

SIGURD.

Sorrows come with ties.

AUDHILD.

Which is harder to bear, think you, an aimless life, or one of sorrow ?

SIGURD.

Oh, an aimless one !

AUDHILD.

Then you are answered.

SIGURD.

But however large a part I might take in matters here, I should not be satisfied. I never.enter a small church without picturing a large one, never a wooden one without longing for those of marble, with their forests of columns and their arched immensity. So I never do a small deed, without thinking of great ones, done in the sight of thousands, in the glow of song.

AUDHILD.

I understand ; with such longings you cannot find rest in Orkney.   .

SIGURD.

If I had but some great aim, I could bear anything, suffer anything!

AUDHILD.

And have you not?

SIGURD.

Know you of what you ask? Have you?

AUDHILD.

A woman —

SIGURD.

True, she awaits hers. I began by putting mine behind me.

AUDHILD.

I had thought an aim in life might be found at any time. [*Sigurd shakes his head.*] Forgive me that I have led your thoughts to this. You depart at once?

SIGURD.

I am now placed as once before. When I came to Scotland my crusader's path was clear before me, and yet I stayed. And every day I yearned — not for the crusade, nor for home, nor for anything definite, but still unceasingly yearned.

AUDHILD.

You will stay.

SIGURD.

You have spoken such words, and so spoken them — I

will stay, until I have thought it over. I now go up to
the hill, to see how matters stand yonder.

AUDHILD.

Take your sword with you.

SIGURD.

That you should remind me of that! Thanks! May
I in return remind you of something?

AUDHILD.

If you will take so much thought for me.

SIGURD.

I hear that you go about the island alone. It is not
safe; I have heard words spoken — for you are fair.
Do not be angered by my counsel: you can forget it.

[*Goes.*

SCENE FOURTH.

AUDHILD. HELGA [*from her son's room, downcast*].

AUDHILD [*falls on her neck*].

I have wounded thee often!

HELGA.

Wilt thou but learn to love, thou wilt be gentler.

[*Audhild kisses her and goes.*

SCENE FIFTH·

HELGA.

HELGA.

I cannot grasp his thought. It is like an affrighted
beast, and hides itself deeper and deeper. Too much
have we done — or too little. We stand midway, and
he now fears both friend and foe. But what if he had
nothing to fear! What if he had no longer need of
Sigurd, of these men, of us even — having no longer a
brother! To do away with the brother! Horrid
thought, how it tempts me! I must speak to Frakark
— no, it is her thought too; I must trust in Sigurd,—
no, he may no longer be depended on; Sven Viking?
But what would I have of him after all. There is now
but one thing — and I dare not do that. I must behold
my son daily wasting away, and may not help him!
Not help him? A mother and not help him? Frakark; yes, Frakark is so strong! There is a chill in her
very look — away with Sigurd! But is she not worse
than Sigurd? Her violence frightens every one away.
But Sigurd, he draws men too closely to him. I would
that light might come from Heaven, for in my mind
there is only darkness.

SCENE SIXTH.

HELGA. FRAKARK [enters].

HELGA.

Hast thou been upon the chapel hill?

FRAKARK.

Yes.   [*She walks about humming softly.*

HELGA.

What means that terrible outcry? Surely no one can be preaching, for they are all speaking at once.

FRAKARK.

Then they must have something serious to talk about.

HELGA.

What dost thou mean? Speak they of us?

FRAKARK.

They do indeed.   [*Singing.*]
"He put forth to sea with full-set sail,
And the waves cast their light on his glistening mail,
    As he stood at the helm!"

HELGA.

Frakark, I am afraid of Sigurd.

FRAKARK.

And I fear him no longer.

HELGA.

Has anything happened?

FRAKARK.

Yes, the people seek to make him earl.

HELGA.

And thou dost not fear him?

FRAKARK.

A handful of traitors !

HELGA.

In whom can we trust ?

FRAKARK [*sings*].

" He put forth to sea with full-set sail "

HELGA.

In ourselves ? Should Torkel Fostre take his part, our power will avail little.

FRAKARK.

Yes ; Torkel Fostre *might* be dangerous.

HELGA.

But he is here and in confinement. Sigurd visits him daily — oh, a deep trap is laid for us !

FRAKARK [*sings*].

" As he stood at the helm " —

HELGA.

Frakark !   Torkel has much to avenge !

FRAKARK.

That he has.

HELGA.

And the day that he is a free man, we are lost !

FRAKARK.

Yes ; the day —

HELGA.

What dost thou mean?

FRAKARK.

That thou art a fool·: Torkel Fostre is slain.

HELGA.

Slain! [*Frakark sings.*] In prison? By whom?
[*Steps nearer to her sister.*] By whom?

FRAKARK.

They suspect me.

HELGA.

Fie!

FRAKARK [*pauses*].

Does that come from thy heart?

HELGA.

Yes, from its depths.

FRAKARK.

It must be shallow to-day.   [*Continues to walk about.*

HELGA.

Frakark! what is to come of all this?

FRAKARK [*sings loudly*].

" And the waves cast their light on his glistening mail."

HELGA.

Ay, and saw their own restless image reflected in it.

But we, who swim after the ship of fate, we must sink, if something does not soon come in sight!

FRAKARK.

I did not reckon upon thy thanks, although the deed has saved us all. Had Torkel Fostre been set free, we should not have had long to swim after the ship of fate.

HELGA.

A living enemy may be won over; a dead one leaves only vengeance behind.

FRAKARK.

Which at the most can but strike a woman, for *thy son, our race,* is now secure.

HELGA.

Dost thou think that Sigurd's men will still bear arms for us?

FRAKARK.

They will rage for a while and make many plans, but soon come to see that without help they dare not revolt, for their numbers are too small.

HELGA.

And Sigurd?

FRAKARK.

Over Torkel's body he will change his mind.

HELGA.

All the threads are slipping from my grasp, so fast

do events follow upon one another. I feel no longer safe; I fear many, and Sigurd most of all.

FRAKARK.

Sigurd departs.

HELGA.

He departs?

FRAKARK.

He is too proud to remain second where for a brief hour he had dreamed of being first.

HELGA.

But when he is gone, who will help us against Earl Paul?

FRAKARK.

Earl Paul? He lies without and has but three ships; he is naught. No, Torkel Fostre — in him was the danger, and it is now done away with.

HELGA.

It is well, then, thinkest thou?

FRAKARK.

I know not when it has been better.

HELGA.

What a terrible noise from the hill! It is increasing; it is still increasing.

SCENE SEVENTH.

The same. AUDHILD.

AUDHILD [*hastily and in terror*].

Helga, Helga, take Harald and fly! The men will
no longer serve you : some will go over to Earl Paul,
others will have Sigurd for a leader ; your life is in
danger !

HELGA.

Dost thou hear, Frakark ?

FRAKARK.

Comest thou from the hill ?

AUDHILD.

Yes, they are all in revolt, all ! When Sigurd ap-
peared, he was received as a king ; they who were about
to seek Earl Paul paused again ; he spoke to the
people —

FRAKARK.

Fished in troubled water.

AUDHILD.

Sigurd stepped forward with noble bearing. He bade
them choose between Earl Harald and them who acted
contrary to Harald's will —

FRAKARK.

So ! So !

AUDHILD.

And the monks still cried about civil strife and hell-fire ; ever about civil strife and hell-fire. The mob was aroused ; some vowed to take the cross, others shouted that the earls must leave the islands, and Sven Viking's voice, higher than all the rest, proclaimed that Sigurd must now take the helm !

HELGA.

My son, my son !

AUDHILD.

And then there was a terrible uproar. I think I saw Sigurd sitting upon his shield, and then, — the storm broke over me, — they shouted, about me and after me, — some, that they would burn our house ; others, that Earl Paul was coming up the fjord. I know not how I came hither. But fly, Helga ; for they will soon break in upon us !

HELGA [*with decision*].

I will depart with my son. So will it be known to all who is guilty of the murder.

FRAKARK.

Do not so, Helga! We should be separated.

HELGA.

When my son is in safety, I will take thought of whom I have left behind.

AUDHILD.

It sounds like the breaking up of ice in a storm. Fly, Helga !

HELGA.

Ay! [*Hastens towards her son's room, and then pauses*]. Sigurd's voice?

AUDHILD.

He might save us yet!

HELGA.

But he will not.

AUDHILD [*as if spellbound*].

Will he not?

SIGURD [*without*].

You, who hold watch by the fjord, send me word of every sail that approaches; you, who hold watch over the house, let no one pass in or out, save at my command.

AUDHILD.

Blessed Olaf, what is this?

FRAKARK.

Are we prisoners in our own house?
                           [*The three women cling together.*

SCENE EIGHTH.

The same. SIGURD [*armed*].

SIGURD.

It must be done quickly! Good, you are both here!
[*Removes his cloak and helmet, steps back, and draws the bolts.*

FRAKARK.

What art thou thinking of?

SIGURD.

That should I rather ask of you.

FRAKARK.

We are fastened in?

SIGURD.

Ay, and the watch stands without.

FRAKARK.

At the other door, too?

SIGURD.

Yes; should you attempt to break out, you are as good as dead.

HELGA.

This is the stranger in whom we trusted!

FRAKARK.

Take heed, Sigurd!

SIGURD.

Because of you, who cannot now take heed for yourselves?

FRAKARK.

We gave our power to an honest man, and find a rebel.

SIGURD.

Give me parchment : there is a treaty of peace to be drawn.

FRAKARK *and* HELGA.

A treaty of peace !

HELGA.

With whom ?

SIGURD.

With Earl Paul.

HELGA.

His power has grown again ?

SIGURD.

Yes.

HELGA.

And thou wilt not fight him ?

FRAKARK.

Dost thou not perceive, he is to be fought with quills ?

HELGA.

Sigurd ! Thou dost not fight him ?

SIGURD.

No !

HELGA.

Now dost thou deem thyself secure. But thou art

such a traitor, Sigurd Slembe, that no power upon earth shall save thee from my vengeance!

SIGURD [*astonished*].

I will show you that I have the upper hand here.

FRAKARK.

Do not think that thou hast conquered us. We can find help, where thou least thinkest!

SIGURD.

Find some higher aim! for this will fail you.

FRAKARK.

Speak not to me of aims, young man, for of ours mine is the higher set.

SIGURD.

What say you? Ah well, it is true. So little is needed. But do not remind me too strongly of it now.

AUDHILD [*stepping forward*].

Tell me; must Helga go?

SIGURD.

She is my prisoner, as are all of you. No one leaves this spot.

AUDHILD.

But Earl Paul is coming.

SIGURD.

Not so far as this.

HELGA.

Not ?

SIGURD.

He waits for my men to stream forth from the assembly and join forces with him.   Instead, he will hear that they have gathered about me.

FRAKARK.

Then it is with thee that we have to deal?

SIGURD.

With me.

FRAKARK.

And thou dost plot with our enemies, with Earl Paul ; now I understand thee !

HELGA.

Hast thou the heart to forget him who sits yonder in his sick-room, and knows naught of danger?

SIGURD.

Go in there yourself !   I no longer share my power and my plans with any one.   You have caused enough misfortune.

AUDHILD.

Oh, you are noble — you will not misuse your power ?

HELGA [*to Frakark*].

Look at Audhild !

SIGURD.

I thought we had spoken together.

AUDHILD.

Yes. *I* trust in you!

FRAKARK [*to Helga*].

Thou art right!

HELGA.

But it is too late now!

FRAKARK.

It is dangerous!

SIGURD [*who has seated himself at the table, rising*].

But I cannot write — my hand —   [*To Audhild.*]
You must help me.

AUDHILD.

I?   But I have never written except for myself.

SIGURD.

Your help now is of much moment to me. [*Firmly.*]
You will not refuse it.

AUDHILD.

If I can be of service to you —

FRAKARK.

Her writing is not good enough to be of use.

SIGURD.

It takes one who can read to judge of that. You
may leave us!

HELGA.

Audhild must come too.

SIGURD.

Audhild has promised to stay.

FRAKARK.

She must obey us; we stand in her mother's stead.

SIGURD.

It is I who command now; and if she do not write, it may fare ill with you all.

FRAKARK.

Come, Helga! When in need, good sometimes flows from evil.

HELGA.

Yes, if they are found together.   [*They go.*

SCENE NINTH.

SIGURD, AUDHILD.

SIGURD.

The people believe that I wish to seize the power; through that belief I can save you all. If I now use my position to quickly arrange a peace between the brothers, all plans of revolt will be thwarted.

AUDHILD.

Then the treaty is in the interest of the brothers.

SIGURD.

Of the brothers. What should I care for these bare islands? I wish for nothing here.

AUDHILD.

Nobly said! [*Sits down to write.*

SIGURD.

Do you sit at ease?

AUDHILD.

Thanks!

SIGURD [*slowly*].

"In the name of the Holy Trinity do we make the following treaty, and pray that the king of Norway may ratify it."

AUDHILD [*questioning*].

The king of Norway?

SIGURD.

His rights must be declared anew; therein is the only safety. [*To himself, as Audhild writes.*] May not the two brothers love one another? I must try those means that the women have not tried — and they have hardly thought of that.

AUDHILD.

"The king of Norway may ratify it."

SIGURD.

"We will rule over the islands together, and dwell together, with a single court."

AUDHILD [*half rising*].

Together, and with a single court?

SIGURD.

They have never been happy when apart. [*Audhild looks at him and writes.*] But they who are likely to stir up strife must away; yes, *she* must away!

AUDHILD [*after a while*].

" A single court."

SIGURD.

" All who were concerned in Torkel Fostre's murder are banished from the islands forever."

AUDHILD.

Frakark, then?

SIGURD.

Yes, she it is whom I mean. [*Audhild writes.*] But the mother shall stay. She must have learned wisdom by this.   [*Pause.*

AUDHILD.

" Forever."ᴸ — No, no, you must not look!

SIGURD.

Surely I must look!

AUDHILD.

But remember, until now I have only written what my own eyes should read.

SIGURD.

Free and clear. Thanks! There is nothing more now, — but for me to go.

AUDHILD.

Jesus! Wherefore?

SIGURD.

Both earls must wish it. Otherwise they could not trust in my treaty.

AUDHILD.

But how can you get away? And your followers?

SIGURD.

As soon as the earls are brought together, I can be spared. I shall have sailed with the crusaders.

AUDHILD.

You said but now, you would reflect upon it.

SIGURD.

I must needs depart. [*Silence, Audhild finishes her writing.*

SIGURD [*thoughtful*].

Thus I shall do my duty. And yet, did I first hold fast the fief, I might more easily win the kingdom, for from hence on some fair day I might sail over the sea's blue carpet to the very throne of Norway. But in any case it would be uncertain. And the Orkneys were too small for me should they not take me to Norway. They would but poorly satisfy my longings. Were there only something here to hold me!

AUDHILD.

Is this all ?

SIGURD.

Yes, I thank you.

AUDHILD.

You go, then ?

SIGURD.

Yes, the counsel I but now gave you must be the last.

AUDHILD.

It was just concerning that —

SIGURD.

You remember, then ?

AUDHILD.

Yes, and to show you that I will heed it — I have a knife; [*takes it from her bosom*] and I no longer have use for it. I wish that you would take it — it has been blessed.

SIGURD.

A noble weapon.

AUDHILD.

It came from Jerusalem. My father brought it thence.

SIGURD.

Now shall it make the journey once more, and go home with me as once with him.

AUDHILD.

May God be with you!

SIGURD.

You go?

AUDHILD.

Yes.

SIGURD.

But not yet?

AUDHILD.

There is nothing more.

SIGURD.

But we have never before really spoken together.

AUDHILD.

And now I think it best that we speak no more together.

SIGURD.

What say you?

AUDHILD.

Nothing.

SIGURD.

Audhild!

AUDHILD.

Farewell!

SIGURD.

Audhild!

AUDHILD.

Sigurd! [*He stretches his arms towards her and she casts herself upon his neck. As in a trance.*] What have I done?

SIGURD.

I know not, but one moment has made me happier than I had thought all my life could make me.

AUDHILD.

You must away.

SIGURD.

But now no more.

AUDHILD.

Your crusaders?

SIGURD.

I know them not.

AUDHILD.

Your plans?

SIGURD.

I have forgotten them.

AUDHILD.

God in heaven, what happiness is mine!

[*They embrace.*

SIGURD.

Audhild!

AUDHILD.

Sigurd!

SIGURD.

Once again, Audhild!

AUDHILD.

Sigurd! Eternal Creator! that thou shouldst love me!

SIGURD.

Look upon me!

AUDHILD.

I do naught else.

SIGURD.

Thou hast tears!

AUDHILD.

I may not stay them.

SIGURD.

Let me kiss thee!

AUDHILD.

Yes.   [*He kisses her.*

SIGURD.

Can this have an end?

AUDHILD.

Not while I hold thee.

SIGURD.

Then loosen thy hair and bind me!

AUDHILD.

Is it indeed thee whom I hold?

SIGURD.

Oh, yes!

AUDHILD.

And is it indeed true that thou lovest me?

SIGURD.

I think it is.

AUDHILD.

It is almost too much to believe.

[*They embrace again.*

SCENE TENTH.

The same. HELGA [*enters*].

SIGURD.

What will you?

HELGA.

The treaty.

SIGURD.

What? The treaty? Here it is.

HELGA.

It provides ?

SIGURD.

No, do not read, but get it signed — quickly !

HELGA.

But I must know the contents.

SIGURD.

No, — yes ; but not here ! Hear me, read it and study it as you will, so that I hear nothing from you ; for, by Olaf, I will have no reflection, nothing but the signature !

HELGA.

I do not know you now !

SIGURD.

No, you do not know me ! You know not who I am, what I deign to do ! No reflection, woman. Bring me the signature at once !

HELGA.

By all the saints ! There must be something in it ! [*Glances at the parchment and cries.*] Shall Frakark away ?

SIGURD.

Yes !

HELGA.

But Frakark ?

SIGURD.

Yes! yes! Do not dare oppose a word! [*Helga goes towards her son's door.*] Yes, I have spoken, yes!   [*She withdraws.*

SCENE ELEVENTH.

SIGURD, AUDHILD.

SIGURD.

These women are so importunate, given to dispute, wearisome! Audhild! Hast thou fled into some corner? Come out again! [*She is silent.*] Audhild! [*She is still silent.*] How changed is thy look!

AUDHILD.

I am afraid of thee!

SIGURD.

Thou art afraid of me?

AUDHILD.

There are two men in thee.

SIGURD.

What dost thou say?

AUDHILD.

That was not thyself.

SIGURD.   *

But, Audhild.

AUDHILD.

Hard as steel springing over the floor with unmeasured step, with evil flashing eyes, and a voice as from some gloomy passage. While thou standest thus, I see it again!

SIGURD.

Only a moment's temper, Audhild. The feelings easily escape their bounds when aroused.

AUDHILD.

But in such fashion?

SIGURD.

Forget it and come forth again!

AUDHILD.

Speak gently to me first!

SIGURD.

I am gentle only when I look at thee. And if there yet remain in me any passion to cause thee terror, believe me, it will vanish when thou shalt blush upon my morning, and smiling bring to me once more the day; call me home and cast a veil over my eventide [*she approaches*], for thou art peace and home to me. Lay thy hands upon my head.

AUDHILD.

Sigurd. Couldst thou ever leave me?

SIGURD.

Never!

AUDHILD.

But this unrest in thee? Who art thou, Sigurd?

SIGURD.

One who forgets who he is.

AUDHILD.

Hast thou done some evil deed?

SIGURD.

No. But question not.

AUDHILD.

In love there is trust. I could tell *thee* all.

SIGURD.

And I thee. But it is not best that thou shouldst know all.

AUDHILD.

Yet it is not well that I should know something to be hidden. Hast thou loved another before me?

SIGURD.

Never.

AUDHILD.

How didst thou come to love me?

SIGURD.

In a moment, I think — I know not how — and thou me?

AUDHILD.

From when I first saw thee; and now I can tell thee, hadst thou departed, I should have died.

SIGURD.

And I was so near to departure !

AUDHILD.

See now !   How different is thy love from mine !

SIGURD.

I, too, am unlike thee.

AUDHILD.

Yes, I cannot grasp it yet ; it is something great, wonderful !   Thou must be some mighty chieftain's son.

SIGURD.

Audhild !

AUDHILD.

What is it ?

SIGURD.

For our future's sake, speak no more of that !

AUDHILD.

My God !

SIGURD.

Nor look thus, Audhild !

AUDHILD.

Look ?   I know not —

SIGURD.

It still asks, Who art thou, Sigurd ?

AUDHILD.

Then do not gaze upon me!

[*She hides her head upon his breast.*

SCENE TWELFTH.

The same. HELGA.

SIGURD.

Again there!

HELGA [*from her son's room*].

Thou must be a wizard, stranger! For thy work has done what mine for three years has not availed to; he rose up and sang. And when he came to what is written about Frakark, he laughed, and called his boy to him. Here is his signature; see what monstrous letters they are!

SIGURD [*taking the treaty*].

Good, — it shall be sent at once.

SCENE THIRTEENTH.

The same. FRAKARK.

HELGA.

But what will Frakark say?

SIGURD.

Ask her: there she is.

HELGA [*calls*].

Frakark!   [*The sisters look at one another. Silence·*

FRAKARK.

What is it?

SIGURD.

I have drawn a treaty of peace between the brothers; among other matters therein is this, that all who were concerned in Torkel Fostre's murder are forever banished from the islands. The treaty bears already Earl Harald's signature. [*Silence.*] It is you who are meant.

FRAKARK.

That, then, is my reward.

SIGURD.

It befits the work. [*Silence.*

FRAKARK [*to Sigurd*].

And thou remainest?

SIGURD.

I leave the islands at the same time. [*Aside and in great confusion.*] But that is no longer my plan.

AUDHILD.

Now thou wilt not do that.

FRAKARK.

Who shall remain with the earl?

HELGA.

No one.

FRAKARK.

No one?

HELGA.

But me. The brothers shall dwell together hereafter.

FRAKARK.

Ha, ha, ha, ha!

HELGA.

Thou art not the only one to be rejoiced at this news.
Harald laughed too.

FRAKARK.

Ha, ha, ha, ha! So, when children build, old folks
get the stones.

HELGA.

Thou shalt see more! [*To Sigurd.*] Let the treaty
be sent to Earl Paul at once! [*Sigurd looks at it, but
does not answer.*] Hast thou changed thy mind again?

SIGURD [*turning from her, to himself*].

All is changed now. My future springs from the
same soil as theirs.

HELGA [*to Audhild*].

Why goes he not? [*To Sigurd.*] Thou wilt depart;
it is thine own wish!

SIGURD.

It was; — but who would push his boat away from
shore, when a woman beckons with white hand, and the
house stands open behind her?

HELGA [*stepping with a cry between them*].

You love one another !

SIGURD.

Yes! [*Going to Audhild's side.*]   And I will depart
no more !

HELGA.

Thou art no longer in my son's service ?   Thou hast
plans of thine own ?

SIGURD.

True; I have other aims now.

HELGA.

And my son shall fall ?

SIGURD.

I work no longer for others.

HELGA.

And thou wilt take what is his ?

SIGURD.

I take what offers.

HELGA.

Jesus Christ!   Where may I look for help now ?

FRAKARK [*forward*].

With me, Helga.   Away from him, Audhild, he is a
traitor to our race !

SIGURD [*reflectively*].

I think I will break loose at once.

HELGA.

If there is in thee the least honor, thou wilt send the treaty !

SIGURD.

Yes, I will break loose !

[*Makes a motion to tear the treaty.*

HELGA.

It is no longer thine ! It bears his hand who sways the land !

SIGURD.

The land is not his : it is the King of Norway's.

FRAKARK.

The feudal claims have not been enforced since the time of Magnus Barfod.

SIGURD.

The brothers are in unlawful possession — and it is time to change that.

FRAKARK.

And that wilt thou take upon thyself ?

SIGURD.

I have a word for the King of Norway, who will give me as a fief what they unjustly hold.

[*Audhild has retired to the background.*

HELGA.

And all the blood that our race has spilt in strife for this unhappy dominion, has it all been shed for a stranger's sake?

SIGURD.

It is ever thus. From the theft of Fafner's gold has stolen wealth brought with it no fortune, only sorrow.

FRAKARK.

But this wealth hast thou undertaken to preserve for us!

SIGURD.

When you slew Torkel Fostre, you broke the pact yourself. To no one here do I owe aught — save to her.
                                           [*Looking towards Audhild.*

HELGA.

Does Audhild stand for the right by which you seize upon my son's land?

SIGURD.

She made me wish to use the right which the arms of my followers gives me. But I have another and a greater right, and of that you shall hear upon the day when I meet the King of Norway.

HELGA.

Art thou then he whom they say? —

SIGURD.

That shall you know in time.

FRAKARK.

Thou seest, Helga, thou seest now what comes of sharing the power with another. And wouldst thou still further share it with thy son's brother?

HELGA.

Oh, Audhild, help me, as thou knowest what it is to love !

AUDHILD [*to Sigurd*].

Sigurd, we might live together without that.

SIGURD.

Must I, then, always be sacrificed ?

AUDHILD.

To renounce what is another's is not to be sacrificed.

SIGURD.

But it is not theirs ! Couldst thou but know : it is mine with far more right than theirs !

AUDHILD.

What now stirs thy soul, I may not divine. Oh, give them the treaty : I will follow thee whither thou wilt!

HELGA.

Hearest thou ? She whom thou hast chosen implores thee, I as a mother implore thee, and he whose entire happiness rests in that treaty implores thee also.

SIGURD [*to himself*].

Well, Earl Paul may come! The two brothers together! The easier are both made prisoners — and sent to the King of Norway. Here is the treaty!

[*Gives it to Audhild.*]

AUDHILD.

Oh, thanks, thanks! Here, Helga.

HELGA.

All the saints be praised! It must off at once.

FRAKARK [*coming towards her*].

Hast thou bethought thyself?

HELGA.

Yes. It is the sole means to save him yet untried.

FRAKARK.

There is one other.

HELGA.

Tempt me not! Earl Paul shall come!

FRAKARK.

But when he comes— [*Helga pauses.*] We will give him the shirt on which I have sewn for three years.

HELGA.

Hush!   [*She leaves.*

AUDHILD.

Sigurd, whither shall we go?

SIGURD.

Meet me in the morning before the others are up.

AUDHILD.

But shall we not depart ?

SIGURD.

That I will tell thee when the brothers have come together.

ACT THIRD.

The hall is decked with shields, skins, and carpets; seats are arranged; servants run in and out. It is dawn; a knot of servants are sitting together and cleaning the silver, Kåre among them, singing.

SCENE FIRST.

KÅRE, SERVANTS.

KÅRE.

What unseen force do the waves obey ?
   What mounts in the west so red ?
What kindles stars in the camp of day
   As torches lit for the dead ?

ALL.

God give thee help, our earl,
God give thee help, our earl,
For 't is Helga, who comes to the Orkneys.

KÅRE.

What dragon is this that speeds so fleet
   O'er the waves struck red with blood,
While the sea-birds flock about my feet
   And screaming skim o'er the flood ?

ALL.

God give thee help, our earl,

God give thee help, our earl,
For 't is Helga, who comes to the Orkneys.

KÅRE.

What radiant maid doth my senses daze?
What wonderful melody?
And why, oh why, do you tearful gaze?
And why do the flowers die?

ALL.

God give thee help, our earl,
God give thee help, our earl,
For 't is Helga, who comes to the Orkneys.

A WINTERCLAD MAN [*at the door*].

Hush! A light is struck in the earl's room!

[*They all rise.*

KÅRE.

He expects his brother to-day.   Are the ships in
sight?

THE MAN.

It is too dark to see yet.

KÅRE.

Well, well, it will soon be day.   [*They leave.*

SCENE SECOND.

THE EARL *and his boy,* SVEN ASLEJVSSON.

THE EARL.

Come, now!   There is no one here.

SVEN.

Hu ! it is so cold here !

THE EARL.

Put something more about thee.   [*He enwraps him.*

SVEN.

Why dost thou wish to stay here ?

THE EARL.

There is more room.

SVEN.

Wilt thou never sleep ?

THE EARL.

Later, I will sleep later.   My brother's ships ought
to be in sight now.

SVEN.

It is too dark to see yet.

THE EARL.

Poor boy, thou art tired.   Watch but this one night
with me !   Thou mayest rest afterwards.   They are still
sewing upon the shirt, sayest thou ?

SVEN.

Yes, both.

THE EARL.

And they speak of my brother as they sew.

SVEN.

All the time.

THE EARL.

All the time. [*Silence.*] Didst thou hear what the men were talking about in the night?

SVEN.

No, not in the night, I was so sleepy.

THE EARL.

But thou heardst the song?

SVEN.

The song, yes.

THE EARL.

It was about my mother, thou sayest.

SVEN.

Yes, and about thy father, who went mad when thy mother came. But he did not do that?

THE EARL.

He was a wise man. But the song, do they all sing it?

SVEN.

They all sing it.

THE EARL.

They all sing it. [*Silence.*] Sven!

SVEN.

Yes.

THE EARL.

They hate us, then, here in the islands?

SVEN.

I do not think you are beloved.

THE EARL.

I will tell thee something to-day that I have long had at heart. I will go hence!

SVEN.

Go? but whither?

THE EARL.

Away from it all — from hatred, from temptation, from all evil things, away !

SVEN.

Then I will go, too.

THE EARL.

Whither I go, none may follow.

SVEN.

But only the great ships go from the Orkneys.

THE EARL.

That is not the only way; it is a discovery, Sven. When thou hast observed me silent, I was thinking it out.

SVEN.

I do not understand thee.

THE EARL.

And yet it is old enough. But each time it must be found anew ; it may not be explained.

SVEN.

And thou hast found it?

THE EARL.

Long since.   It was the knowledge of it which for-
bade me to resist, for I knew well that I might fall
back upon it.   It was that which made me patient, for
I knew that I might go if things went too ill with me.
And now are things much too ill with me — they would
kill my brother!

SVEN.

Thou goest, then?

THE EARL.

Over the great waters, the sea shall take me and hide
me.

SVEN.

Nay, do not go! for my sake, do not go!

THE EARL.

For thy sake, too, must I go.   Thou hast been with
me too long.   A great future awaits thee; I would not
stand in thy way.

SVEN.

Thou standest in the way of none.

THE EARL.

Of all, even of myself.   My life is to me a burden,
to others an object of scorn and hatred, and to my own
mother a temptation.   She has done much evil for my

sake, and now for my sake will she kill my brother. Why should he die? Is it not better that I, who am nothing worth, should go, than he, who is strong and a man of deeds? And shall I not spare my mother the sin? And shall I not give to thee a future, my beloved boy?

SVEN.

If thou dost leave me, I shall have nothing more to live for.

THE EARL.

Thou art young, thou wilt soon be happy again.

SVEN.

Oh, never!

THE EARL.

Yes, when thou art home in thy father's house again, and knowest that it is well with thy poor sick earl where he is, thou wilt confess that thou art happy.

SVEN.

But whither wilt thou go?

THE EARL.

Hush!

SVEN.

Will thy dogs go with thee?

THE EARL.

Thou shalt have them. They were howling last night. Thou must be kind to them.

SVEN.

And wilt thou leave us at once?

THE EARL.

I know not, and did I know, I should not tell thee. Do not weep, little Sven!

SVEN.

Oh, wilt thou never look upon me again?

THE EARL.

Yes, at night-tide, in thy dreams. I think I may promise that, for I know that I have thus been with my brother. And then I will speak with thee as now, and tell thee when danger threatens, and help thee bear those thoughts that are too heavy for one alone.

SVEN.

But wilt thou not come in the daytime, too?

THE EARL.

A bird of night have I been and must remain; I have never known the daytime. Do not weep, little Sven! How kind thou hast been to me! And now I thank thee for it all. [*Kisses him.*] And so we must part!

SVEN.

No, no!   [*Throws himself upon Harald's neck.*

THE EARL.

For to-day, I mean. Be patient, my beloved boy!
[*Weeps himself.*

SVEN.

No, thou biddest me farewell; thou wilt not go without my knowing it?

THE EARL.

No, no —

SVEN.

Oh, take me with thee!

THE EARL.

Hush! For thee are great things in store. Thou shalt fare far abroad, and mighty deeds shall praise thee; foes shall rise up and fall again before thy sword; conquering shalt thou fulfil all that I have left thee to do, and then only shalt thou follow me. Go out now and breathe strength with the morning air!

SVEN.

But thou wilt call me when thou art ready to go?

THE EARL.

That I promise thee. [*Going to the door with him.*] Now it is day, and I must go back to my room, and be alone. Farewell!

SVEN [*upon his neck*].

Oh, earl, how I love thee!

THE EARL.

Thanks, thanks!
[*He kisses Sven in return, and gently pushes him out at the door.*

SCENE THIRD.

THE EARL [*alone*].

So ! The hardest is over. They may come now. I
will go to my room and wait with the door half-open.
And when they come, I will for once arouse their conscience.   [*Goes in at the left.*

SCENE FOURTH.

AUDHILD [*from the right*].

Ah, I am always the first. But if I were not, I
should be ashamed. He must be here soon, for I saw
them carrying lights about down at the ship-houses.
The day is not far off ; and when its first rays kiss the
snow, he will — [*Hides her face.*] I will pray till he
comes ; I am forgetting it of late. I woke up last night
when the earl's dogs howled so piteously ; I was afraid
and tried to pray. But the moment a door opened I
found myself listening for Sigurd's step ; if the watchman but coughed, I was beside myself, for I thought that
Sigurd was waiting. Oh, ye blessed men and women, be
not angry with me that I forget you for him ! I know
it is wrong, but I cannot help it. Now I will make
amends and pray till he comes. [*Kneels.*] Yet not to
you, ye stern saints in the church, but to thee, thou
blessed Olaf, to thee who didst take the golden-haired
Astrid to thy embrace, — although it was not wholly fitting, — thou must know what lovers suffer, and how they
are beset by manifold temptations, and give way to them,
and forget you, ye saints, and all that is, and afterwards
atone for it with a lifetime of tears. But be not thus

stern with me, for my plight is most piteous ! I cannot
hold fast the man whom I love. I live in continual fear
lest the next day take him from me ; I surely cherish
him more than I ought, for he is far above me, but still
must I pray that he be mine! For how noble he is ! I
went about and would not perceive it ; but even when I
turned away from him I felt his radiant presence near ;
I was persuaded that I would not love, and so came to
love far too well — oh, forgive me, for how noble he is !
His very wrath, is it not like wave rolling upon wave ;
his speech, does it not rouse the thoughts as the birds are
aroused when the huntsman strikes into the forest; his
walk, is it not soft as an echo in a summer night, and are
not his movements like the tones of a martial song ; the
speech of his eyes, is it not whispered through the air
as the wind in the tree-tops ! But this is not prayer !
I am deep bowed down with shame, for his image dis-
places yours, ye holy men and women. Hush, he himself is here !

SCENE FIFTH.

SIGURD [*at the principal door*]. AUDHILD.

SIGURD.

I am here !

AUDHILD.

But see : I was the first !

SIGURD.

It is because I lay awake longer than thou last night ;
I thought of thee.

AUDHILD.

But the love that keeps watch for desire is stronger than that which is kept awake by memories.

SIGURD.

Ah, when I sleep, my sleep is filled with dreams of thee, and so I am loth to wake when morning comes.

AUDHILD.

But I love better, for my dreams of thee are so vivid that they wake me.

SIGURD.

No, Audhild, I love thee better, for now is dream and reality one for me, and I know no longer when I sleep and when I am awake.

AUDHILD.

I love thee still more, for away from thee I cannot sleep at all.

SIGURD.

Now thou hast lost, for thou art never away from me.

AUDHILD.

No, I have won, for not even the thought of thee will fill thy place.

SIGURD.

Ah, thou art my thought !

AUDHILD.

Let us exchange, then, that we may round out each other's joy.

SIGURD.

Thou hast so blossomed in these happy days that thou mightest go with me to Provence and be queen of love there.

AUDHILD.

If I am but thine, I have all the crown I desire.

SIGURD.

How joyous thou art!

AUDHILD.

Because thou hast never looked so lovingly upon me.

SIGURD.

Why, thinkest thou?

AUDHILD.

Thou hast resolved to depart?

SIGURD.

No.

AUDHILD.

Shall we not go, then?

SIGURD.

Whither?

AUDHILD.

To Scotland.

SIGURD.

I am tired of Scotland.

AUDHILD.

To England.

SIGURD.

I have fought against her.

AUDHILD.

To Normandy.

SIGURD.

I might find some of my countrymen.

AUDHILD.

Sigurd, I am afraid!

SIGURD.

We can stay where we are.

AUDHILD.

But thou hast banished thyself!

SIGURD.

If I but stretch out my hand, I am earl here.

AUDHILD.

Our happiness must not be built upon others' distress.

SIGURD.

It would do the earls a good turn to end their lord-
ship, and the land a still better one.

AUDHILD.

My soul is troubled at the thought.   Didst thou hear
Harald's dogs in the night?

SIGURD.

No.   But let us talk of our love.

AUDHILD.

We live a venturesome life ; our love consumes itself.

SIGURD.

It rejoices when it knows that danger is near.

AUDHILD.

Thou art like him who gazes upon the sea, thy look is fixed in its depths.

SIGURD.

The happiness of these latter days is so greatly like the sea.

AUDHILD.

But if it bear the enemy's ships against thee, thou must needs look up.

SIGURD.

That the ships are an enemy's is not certain, but certain it is that thou art now sitting by my side.

AUDHILD.

Canst thou then think of but one thing at a time ?

SIGURD.

I can, but will not.   For if I would, I should not be sitting here.

AUDHILD.

What sayest thou ?

SIGURD.

Now thou hast that look again!

AUDHILD.

Oh no! [*She hides her face in his bosom.*] Sigurd! [*She blinds his eyes with her hands.*] See
nothing but my love!

SIGURD.

And it is for that thou dost blind me?

AUDHILD.

I must do it.   Oh, the day when some great thought
comes to thee, then wilt thou leave me!

SIGURD.

Impossible : for just such a thought came with thy
love ; I had once more an aim.

AUDHILD.

It is just that which makes me afraid, for love is not
all thy thought.

SIGURD.

No, it has noble company, earls' company!

AUDHILD.

Sigurd, Sigurd, thou dost wish for more than me alone.

SIGURD.

Love broadens life.

AUDHILD.

It is that!   Oh, thou wilt leave me at last!

SIGURD [*embraces her*].

Childishness ! Dost thou not see, all that we say goes in a circle, which must be closed with a kiss.

[*He kisses her.*

AUDHILD.

How happy I am ! [*Knocking is heard. Starting up.*] The earl's ships are in sight !

SIGURD.

Not yet.

AUDHILD.

But when they are ?

SIGURD.

You will hear it from all about, when they are in sight. [*Knocking heard again.*] The watch would speak with me.

AUDHILD.

Shall I make ready for a journey ?

SIGURD.

Wait till I shall tell thee further.

AUDHILD.

Sigurd, what is thy meaning ?

SIGURD.

Trust to me !

AUDHILD.

I cannot go ; I know not whither to go. [*Bursts into tears.*] Oh, let me stay with thee !

SIGURD.

That cannot be; I have much to see to. [*Knocking heard.*]   Yes, yes!

AUDHILD.

Oh, Sigurd, do not forsake me!

SIGURD.

How canst thou think it, child? [*He leads her to the door.*]   Good morning! [*In the doorway.*]   Good morning!   [*He opens the principal door.*

SCENE SIXTH.

SVEN VIKING [*winterclad*], SIGURD.

SIGURD.

Forgive me, I made thee wait.

SVEN.

We do not see the ships yet; but it is to be done as agreed?

SIGURD.

Certainly.

SVEN.

So, when thou shalt give the signal?

SIGURD.

You are to take the earls captive; but cautiously.

SVEN.

Frakark tried once more to send a message over to Caithness yesterday. [*Smiles.*

SIGURD [*smiles*].

So.

SVEN.

But he to whom she gave the money drank it up. [*Laughs.*

SIGURD [*laughs*].

So.

SVEN.

The crusader ships set forth to-day.

SIGURD.

Ah, that is why there were lights down at the ship-houses last night.

SVEN.

Yes, they think that thou wilt go too. [*Laughs.*

SIGURD [*laughs*].

So. [*They look at one another for a moment. Sven is about to go.*] Thou, Sven!

SVEN.

Well?

SIGURD.

Thou must not act before I give the signal.

SVEN.

No, no.

SIGURD.

Even if it come a little late.

SVEN.

Good.   [*Goes.*

SIGURD [*looking after him*].

I will go down to the crusaders.   For it may yet be
that I depart with them.   [*Goes.*

SCENE SEVENTH.

*The door to the right is slowly opened: the two sisters enter. Fra-
kark carries the shirt.*

FRAKARK, HELGA.

FRAKARK.

The ships are not yet in sight; but we must hasten,
while we are still left alone.   Hast thou the ointment?

HELGA.

Here.

FRAKARK.

Only on the inside.   If a grain of it get on thy fin-
ger —   [*They take up the shirt and turn it inside out.*

HELGA.

Yes, I know it.

FRAKARK.

The shirt is fair without : he loves gold and jewels ;
he will eagerly put it on.
                    [*They hold the shirt with a cloth, and apply the ointment by
                                   means of another.*

HELGA.

Thou settest a trap for the wolf who is to come, while the other is already in the house.

FRAKARK.

Sigurd will reflect at sight of Earl Paul's body.

HELGA.

He did not at sight of Torkel's.

FRAKARK.

It is not the single attempt that terrifies, but the calm repetition. Spread thinner, Helga.

HELGA.

Yes, it must not be seen.

FRAKARK.

This poison is a fine invention.

HELGA.

Whose was it?

FRAKARK.

Some woman's, surely, who was faithless.

HELGA.

Why faithless?

FRAKARK.

Such have the deepest thoughts — and are silent.

HELGA.

It comforts me to think that he will die at once and painlessly.

FRAKARK.

And be far happier than he is now.

HELGA.

May he who survives be that also !

FRAKARK.

He may yet be happy — alone.

HELGA.

I hope he may. One of the brothers must die. I am very calm now.

FRAKARK.

When Maddad's race shall rule the Orkneys and Caithness, our task will be accomplished, Helga.

HELGA.

I will build a chapel here on the island. The roof of the old one is rotten.

FRAKARK.

I have often thought — yes, there on the wrist — that thy son ought to take the cross when all was done. It will arouse him; his father did thus when Magnus was slain.

HELGA.

Yes, thou sayest well.

FRAKARK.

By taking the cross one may blot out his own sins and those of others.

HELGA.

Not of others, I think.

FRAKARK.

I have heard so, — yes, in the sleeve, wherever it comes closest to the body, — but the monks often promise more than they can fulfil.

HELGA.

They will do much for gold.

FRAKARK.

I have spoken with the bishop in Kirkevåg. He is a reasonable man, from whom it is easy to get absolution.

HELGA.

The ointment is almost gone.

FRAKARK.

Then we must have spread it too thick. He will die all the easier.

HELGA.

He has caused us much sorrow.

FRAKARK.

And more was in store.

HELGA.

Had I known what I know now, this should have been done three years ago.

FRAKARK.

I proposed it.

HELGA.

Yet, much would have been different.

FRAKARK.

But our old age will be peaceful now.

HELGA.

And I am weary.   I need peace.

FRAKARK.

We must live here in Orfjara; the sea lends our thought seriousness.

SCENE EIGHTH.

The same.   HARALD [*enters in light morning dress*].

HELGA.

Good day, my son !

HARALD.

Would that I might say as much to you.   That is a singular garment.

FRAKARK.

It is a gift of welcome for thy brother.

HARALD.

It will be welcome indeed since made by your own hands. It would have cost another much toil to make such a shirt.

FRAKARK.

Well ; it has cost us three years of it.

HARALD.

Three years. Much good may be done in three years. How long did Jesus Christ go about with his disciples ?

HELGA.

I do not know.

HARALD.

Three years — it is a sacred number. Karl the Great did much in three years. Saint Olaf converted all southern Norway. It took William less to conquer England, and Alexander half the world. And in three years I have done nothing — while you have worked this shirt. Can a man make up for three years in a single day ?

HELGA.

If a man have given three years to thought, and with each year become more unhappy, he may attempt it, some day.

HARALD.

If a man have given three years to thought, and with each year become more unhappy, he may attempt it some day, — thou didst say the same thing three days ago.

HELGA.

It may be.

HARALD.

And I said : strange how our thoughts meet, I said.

HELGA.

Thou didst indeed.

HARALD.

And again to-day.

HELGA.

What meanest thou, my son ?

HARALD.

It is three years' toil ; and for three years I have done no toil. If I should put it on could I put three years of toil upon me ?

HELGA.

There is no meaning in what thou sayest.

FRAKARK.

The shirt is for thy brother.

HARALD.

It would make a rare penitent's robe for me.

HELGA.

Thou dost not know of what thou speakest !

HARALD.

Hear my dogs, poor beasts !   Give me the shirt !

BOTH.

Take care!

HARALD.

If I put it on, you can see better how it will fit Paul.

HELGA.

Do not touch it!

FRAKARK.

The color will come off!

HARALD.

It must be from your hands, then, for the stuff is not homespun.

HELGA.

Thy dogs are howling.

HARALD.

Yes, piteously.   Give me the shirt!   [*Tries to take it.*

HELGA.

It concerns thy life!

HARALD.

Now thou dost jest.

HELGA.

Is it not thou who dost jest?

HARALD.

Life, mother, life.   Three years of toil are asked to dance for an hour.   Earl Paul shall see from his ship!

BOTH.

What does he say?

HARALD.

I have never begged you for anything, that I can remember, but now I do beg you for this shirt. I have fallen in love with it, as the smoke with the bosom of the air, the leaves of autumn with the earth, the dew of evening with the grass, or a wounded deer with his covert.

FRAKARK.

What madness is this?

HARALD.

I long for this shirt! It is not on account of the color, for that speaks of blood ; nor the pearls, for they speak of the treacherous sea ; nor the gold, for that speaks of the fires of hell. But it is for the three years inwoven like good thoughts in an evil deed, like sense in the speech of a madman, like Daniel at Nebuchadnezzar's feast. Give me the shirt, that I may put myself within it, — only a moment, for a man's light lasts no longer than that. What great thing will you do with it, women? Is there aught greater than to give comfort to a child or light to a man's soul?

HELGA.

Harald, spare us!

HARALD.

Ah, mother, it is all jest, merely jest. Is there anything more amusing than the fox who fears his own shadow; or the avaricious woman who so loads down her boat, that it sinks with her midway; or a she-tiger who finds that she has slain her young with her caresses; or the ambitious man who dies the day before he shall be crowned? So have I seen life miss its aim, and now at the last do I see death fail of its aim also.

BOTH.

But Harald, what is it?

HARALD.

Hush, hush! My finger, the one that touched your shirt, now tingles, burns; it is pregnant with a secret; now, I hold it to my ear, and it tells me, oh, you shall know — here is the shirt!

> [*With a bound he reaches the table and seizes the shirt, which the women have forgotten at sight of his finger, runs with it to his room and bars the door.*

SCENE NINTH.

The two sisters alone [*crying to him*].

HELGA.

The shirt is poisoned! My son, poison!

FRAKARK.

It is for thy brother, insensate!

HELGA.

Thou dost give thyself up to eternal torments!

FRAKARK.

And all of us together!

HELGA.

Before the merciful Almighty's face I fall down upon my knees and pray Him and thee! I who first gave thee life, and a thousand times gave it thee anew at the risk of mine, I, I, it is I who pray! If thou dost leave me there remains but darkness and terror and dearth of heaven all the world around!

FRAKARK.

Do not put it on!

HELGA.

Do not put it on! Do not put it on!

FRAKARK.

He is doing it, he is doing it!

[*She tears the cap from her head.*

HELGA [*rising*].

Thou fearful, accursed spectre of some evil spirit, it is thou who hast done this! Colder than the winter night's wind, more deadly than the marsh vapors, thou hast wrought upon my soul. Through my only weakness, through my love for this child borne by me in shame, thou hast overpowered and misused me! See now thy work! Magnus, Håkon, Torkel, my son, and soon myself, all slain about thee, while thou dost stand there as a tombstone whose inscription tells the manner of our death! There he comes! [*She falls.*

SCENE TENTH.

The same. HARALD [*in the shirt*].

HARALD.

Well, mother, didst thou fall !

FRAKARK.

Let us help her to her feet again.

HARALD.

She will but fall once more.

FRAKARK.

Now it is out !

HARALD.

Ay, it is out ! And now it is ill that all the springs
are frozen, for I burn in hell-fire. So it was this you
had prepared for him ; — what must be prepared for
you? Help me ! I did not know it was so horrible !
My brother, my brother, my brother, couldst thou see
me now ! Let me but bear it to the end and die like a
man, unbent ! [*Shrieks.*] No, no, no, I cannot bear
it !   [*Falls. Helga rises.*

FRAKARK.

There is nothing in the world can help him now.

HARALD.

Yes, something — oh, what torments ! Mother, thou
art the nearest to it !

HELGA.

What is it?

HARALD.

Or Sven, call for Sven! It blazes, it burns, it hisses, it crackles. Oh, oh, give me water!

FRAKARK [*bringing water*].

Here, here!

HARALD.

No, thou give it me, mother! [*She gives it, he drinks.*] A moment's relief! [*Looks at his mother.*] Poor mother! So this draught at death's hour was all thou shouldst give me. Oh, it comes again with licking tongues of flame; call Sven! [*He calls.*] Sven, Sven!

SCENE ELEVENTH.

The same. SVEN ASLEJVSSON [*enters with a knife in his hand*].

SVEN.

Thou dost call, earl! The shirt! Poison!

HARALD.

Give me thy knife!

SVEN.

Earl, earl!   [*He falls to the ground.*

HARALD.

Come not near me! It will be thy death! Thy knife, thy knife! [*He takes it and stabs himself.*]

Now it will soon be over. [*Sven takes it back and lifts up Harald's head.*] Sven, take care of my dogs !

SVEN.

Yes.

HARALD.

And ask my brother to have masses said for me.

SVEN.

Yes.

HARALD.

How everything changes ! Is it thou standing there ?

HELGA.

No, it is I.

HARALD.

Is it thou ?

HELGA.

Oh, look at me !

HARALD.

I see thee not.

HELGA.

Here I am, here ! Oh, canst thou forgive me !

HARALD.

Who is holding my head ?

SVEN.

It is I, — Sven.

HARALD.

Is it Sven?   Where art thou, mother?

HELGA.

I am holding thy hand now.

HARALD.

Look out for the shirt, mother!

HELGA.

No, Harald, I will die with thee.

HARALD.

This is the first time thou hast ever understood me, mother.   Where art thou?

HELGA.

It is I who kiss thee now.

HARALD.

How light it grows!   Is it thou all white?

HELGA.

Here is no one in white.

HARALD.

Yes, there is some one.   Lay me down!   [*It is done.*]   Mother, where art thou?

[*She throws herself upon him.*

SVEN [*rising*].

He is dead.

SCENE TWELFTH.

The same. SIGURD *enters.*

SIGURD.

Dead !

SVEN.

By his own hand.

SIGURD.

Lord Jesus !   [*He tries to raise him up.*

SVEN.

Do not touch the shirt ! It is poisoned.

SIGURD.

Poisoned ?

SVEN.

It was worked for Paul, but he put it on.

SIGURD [*thunderstruck*].

He did 'that ! And I ?   [*Covers his face with his hands.*

SCENE THIRTEENTH.

The same. SVEN VIKING [*with several followers*].

SVEN VIKING.

Earl Paul's ships are in sight now.

SIGURD.

And Earl Harald's have reached their haven.

SVEN VIKING.

He is dead !

THE OTHERS.

Dead !

SIGURD.

Yes, by his own hand ! [*Throws down his cloak.*]
Bear him away in this cloak, for the shirt he wears is
poisoned.

SVEN VIKING [*passing by Sigurd to take hold of the body*].

One of them is out of the way.

SIGURD [*deeply moved, forward*].

Hear me, O God Almighty, who hast warned me ;
the other brother shall sail away in peace !

HELGA [*to the men who are spreading out the cloak*].

Carefully !   Carefully !

SVEN VIKING.

He knows no more of suffering.

HELGA [*who has arisen, and made a sign calling for the attention of
the bystanders*].

Frakark !   The house thou wouldst have built has
fallen in upon us all.   Thou alone art spared, and the
worst fate thou canst know is thine : thou shalt live
longer than thy plans.   Ye others, pray for me !
Pray that the love which brought death upon me may

plead for me with the Source of all love. I follow him still further, whom in life I have sought to know; but let many masses be said for me; for it may be that love alone will not suffice to reunite us. Farewell!

[*The men go out bearing the dead, Helga follows.*]

SIGURD [*to the boy Sven*].

And thou, my little friend, whither wilt thou?

SVEN.

I will go with them until he is buried.

SIGURD.

And then?

SVEN.

I will take his dogs and row home.

SIGURD.

Thou hast served him faithfully, and put many to shame.

SVEN.

I thank you.

SIGURD.

Is not this knife thine?

SVEN.

Ay.

[*He takes it, looks at it, then looks quietly at Frakark, and goes.*]

SIGURD [*to her*].

There grows the man who shall be thy bane.

FRAKARK.

Hast thou more to say to me?

SIGURD.

No.

FRAKARK.

Then I will leave thee alone.   [*She goes.*

SCENE FOURTEENTH.

SIGURD.

I am left alone — in this house — between his corpse
and their broken hopes — face to face with my own.
This silence — this silence following, staring at me like
an enormous eye — all I look upon is plunged in it, and
eternity is round about me.   I hear above me a rushing
as of mighty wings ; for He is here, the great, angry
God.   He has spared me, but how shall I now creep
away and hide myself?   The warning set in my path
was so great, so terrible.   Crushed in spirit I bow down
before Thee ; nevermore shall the hope of power tempt
me!   If I may not serve others, as I have learned but
now ; and as Thou hast not granted that I pursue my
own ends, I here devote myself to thy service, Thou
Ruler of the world, — not in ambition, as once before,
but entirely, and with every thought, and the deed of
every moment yet unborn!   And make Thou this vow
to be, more than a gleam cast by thy angry lightnings
in my soul ; make it to be a lasting light upon my path!
Deep below me now sinks all that has cursed my life,
and my ardor raises me up to Thee, as the disciples to

thy son. Free from all burdens, my soul aspires to Thee; do Thou unfold the banner of the cross, and where it waves, there will I fight to the glory of thy name. What are all things earthly save vapors, spread abroad and drawn in with every breath! How my soul has vainly vexed itself with selfish aims, which come and go! Thy cross is not heavy upon my shoulder; but heaviest of all things known to me is that emptiness of soul which seeks for what I have sought hitherto. Oh, hear me, thou Cross-bearer; I am with Thee while it is day; make but Thou the day to last, so that no night come between us more.

AUDHILD [*is heard calling*].

Oh, this house of horrors! Where art thou, Sigurd? Sigurd, where art thou? [*She enters.*

SCENE FIFTEENTH.

SIGURD, AUDHILD.

AUDHILD.

What has happened? Helga lies dead upon her son's body; the doors are all open; strangers break in upon us. Earl Paul is coming, and Frakark rows away. Where shall I find refuge save with thee, my eternally beloved one?

SIGURD.

Then dost thou seek it with an outlaw!

AUDHILD.

Take me with thee.

SIGURD.

A wife is for peace and the home, but I have no place where I may stay.

AUDHILD.

Thou wilt leave me?

SIGURD.

The dawn has broken in upon our embraces; the house shall be cleansed; now must each seek his own.

AUDHILD.

Eternal God! What, then, will become of me?

SIGURD.

Ask, rather, what I have given thee.

AUDHILD.

Sigurd!

SIGURD.

Sorrow and trembling; an hour of rapture, another of weeping.

AUDHILD.

But what, then, art thou, Sigurd, that I have never felt myself at ease with thee?

SIGURD.

Magnus Barfod's son, and heir to Norway!

AUDHILD.

Thou shouldst not then have spoken to me.

SIGURD.

I have in vain sought peace through all the world, and it was sweet to me when thou didst offer it. I have robbed thee of thine, but have won none for myself. Child, how much ill I have wrought thee!

AUDHILD.

Fear and trembling thou first gavest me. Didst thou appear, I might hardly breathe. What since hath been I know not; it flits before my eyes like a vision of air and sea. I have never been truly awake since then.

SIGURD.

We have learned of late that one may not be so much to another.

AUDHILD.

But what is then to come?

SIGURD.

That which is now past brought no content — we must seek it in the future. I go upon crusade!

AUDHILD.

O Christ! And I shall remain as before — alone!

SIGURD.

Even more alone, — and I, who am the cause of it all, may not help thee, — I am the restless one who brings but evil in return for good. I am the outcast, who may find no peace — save with Thee alone, my God and Father!

AUDHILD.

Do not sorrow; for I would not spare a single hour of those that I have passed in anxious joy with thee. But tell me, thou mighty one, that thou hast loved none save me alone.

SIGURD.

I will tell thee more: in all my life I will love none other.

AUDHILD.

Then will I think of thee as my noble husband, away upon a journey.

SIGURD.

But thou must not forget that he will hardly come back to thee.

AUDHILD.

O Sigurd, Sigurd!

SONG OF THE CRUSADERS [*is heard from the sea*].
> Fair is the earth,
> Fair is God's heaven,
> Fair is the pilgrim path of the soul;
> Singing we go
> Through the fair realms of earth
> Seeking the way to our heavenly goal!

SIGURD [*as the song begins*].

Dost thou hear the song of the crusaders? Once again it lifts me above all doubts and dreams, but higher than before. And let these tones, gliding through the

air like white-robed angels, be our mighty bridal song!
Audhild, farewell! [*They embrace for the last time;
he tears himself away.*] Yes, I come, I come!

[*Departs.*

AUDHILD.

Lord, be with him! [*On her knees.*] But remain
with me also!

PART THIRD.

SIGURD'S RETURN.

CHARACTERS.

SIGURD SLEMBE.

King HARALD GILLE, *his half-brother.*

KOLL SÆBJÖRNSON,
TJOSTULV ÅLESON, } *chieftains of the king.*

HALLKELL HUK.

BEJNTEJN,
SIGURD STALLAR, } *brothers: king's men.*
GYRD,

IVAR KOLLBEJNSON, *chief of the king's men.*

IVAR INGEMUNDSON, *poet.*

ERLEND.

A WATCHMAN.

A NUN

A FINNISH MAIDEN.

FOLLOWERS, CITIZENS, *etc.*

Time — 1136 and the three following years.

ACT FIRST.

The king's court at Bergen. The hall is decked for a feast. Entrance forward on the [spectator's] right. In the centre, on a dais, the throne with a table before it. Harald Gille sits on the throne; his marshal is at the table opposite him, but seated upon a lower level. Upon each side of the king a page, holding a lighted candle. The king's men sit on benches along the side walls; before them are tables laden with food and drink; waiters run back and forth; when they offer anything to the king they fall upon their knees. Gyrd is master of the feast for the day. The scene is one of great magnificence.

SCENE FIRST.

THE KING, KOLL SÆBJÖRNSON, HALLKELL HUK, TJOSTULV ÅLESON, IVAR INGEMUNDSON, BEJNTEJN, GYRD, SIGURD STALLAR, IVAR KOLLBEJNSON, *and many others. A low conversation is going on.*

TJOSTULV ÅLESON

[*rises from his seat and goes towards Ivar Ingemundson, who sits at the right in the foreground. Tjostulv draws a stool forward and sits down by him*].

You know him then?

IVAR INGEMUNDSON.

Not himself, but his career.

TJOSTULV.

They were hard words that we heard spoken of him. Do you believe them true?

IVAR.

It was very quiet here afterwards. So I think that his fate is sealed.

TJOSTULV.

Bejntejn must have crossed him before. No man speaks thus without a sense of injury.

IVAR.

Bejntejn seeks to be the first man in the land. But Sigurd conquered him when a boy.

TJOSTULV.

Aha! Then Sigurd comes at an ill-chosen hour, for Bejntejn and his kin —

IVAR.

You are overheard!

TJOSTULV.

How long has Sigurd been on crusade?

IVAR.

Eight full years.

TJOSTULV.

And since then?

IVAR.

Since then he has cruised for two years in the North Sea, between Denmark, Iceland, and Normandy.

TJOSTULV.

As a merchant?

IVAR.

As a merchant.

TJOSTULV.

He has been uncertain of himself.

IVAR.

He has been that all his life.

TJOSTULV.

And he comes at an unfortunate time.

IVAR.

The king knows of whom we are speaking.　　.

GYRD [*in a low voice to Tjostulv*].

The king does you the honor of drinking with you.
[*Tjostulv hastens back to his place, and rises, holding a beaker to his breast, with head bowed, until the king has drunk.*

THE KING.

Hail, thou !

GYRD [*calls*].

The king drinks !
[*All drop what they have in their hands, bow their heads, and fold their hands, until the king has drunk.*

HALLKELL HUK.

May I be allowed, my lord, to resume the subject of which we last spoke ; I would fain ask Koll Sæbjörnson, who comes but now from the Orkneys, of the murder of Torkel Fostre.　Who has answered for it ?

KOLL.

It is now ten years old.

HALLKELL.

That I know, and also that the slain man was your friend. Was not Sigurd Slembe guilty of that murder?

KOLL.

He was then chief in power upon the islands ; more I know not.

HALLKELL.

If he was chief in power, it behooves him to answer for it. What think you, my lord, of calling him to account? It might give him other matter to think upon than the sharing of your kingdom.

SEVERAL VOICES.

Ay. Hallkell is right!

THE KING [*whose speech and pronunciation are somewhat foreign.*

Let — let us talk of something else. [*To Hallkell.*]
Hail, thou!   [*They all bow their heads as before.*

TJOSTULV.

Take it not ungraciously, my lord, that we would fain ward off this danger. For it may hardly be doubted that Sigurd is the son of Magnus Barfod; he bears the proof upon his brow. He now in all respect demands an answer, and that must he have. And that the answer should not consort with his wish is hardly to be counseled, for strife would surely then arise.

HALLKELL.

But there are not many sitting here who can desire that it *shall* consort with his wish.

GYRD.

The way out of the difficulty, offered by Hallkell, does not seem to me ill advised.

SEVERAL VOICES.

No, it is not ill advised.

TJOSTULV.

It seems to me both dangerous and unjust. It is a shame thus to counsel the king, who is so good of heart.

THE KING.

Marshal, have we no gift for Tjostulv?

THE MARSHAL.

The gifts which we last got are all—

THE KING.

Take this beaker!

> [*He gives it to the marshal and takes another; the marshal hands it to Tjostulv.*

TJOSTULV [*standing*].

Many think this with me, that you are the most gracious king in the North.

> [*The beaker is passed around amid cries and exclamations.*

GYRD [*calls*].

The king drinks!   [*All do as before.*

HALLKELL.

We were speaking of the Orkneys. Can you not, Koll Sæbjörnson, tell us something of the Orkneys ? As you have but now come from them, you must have news unknown to the most of us.   [*The king nods assent to Koll.*

KOLL.

Since the king, our lord, welcomes the suggestion, it becomes to me a duty. You, lord, bestowed men and ships upon my son, and so the subjugation of the land was undertaken. Earl Paul was made prisoner by a cunning man whose name is Sven Aslejvsson, and the Orkneys fell to the rule of my son, — and thus became once more a fief of Norway. [*Rising.*] It is, then, my lord, a happy day for me that I may thank you for the grace granted to me and to my son, although we were the most unworthy of all. And the lordly men I see here about me surely feel as I do, that in the Orkneys the crown has won back a great possession, and that more through report of the great goodness and graciousness of our king than through strife, which it is ever best to avoid. The Blessed Virgin Mary and Saint Olaf will pray for you every day. May the love of your subjects and your wonted fortune follow you until your last hour — which we pray may be far off, for the sake of this kingdom, and for our sakes also, who are nearest you !

ALL [*rising*].

Fortune be with the king !

THE KING.

Marshal, hast thou no gift for Koll ?

THE MARSHAL.

The gifts which we last got are all —

THE KING.

Then take these cushions from my seat.

[*They take the cushions upon which he has been sitting, and give them to Koll.*

ALL [*to one another*].

What liberality !   What goodness of heart !

[*The cushions are passed around.*

KOLL [*rising*].

There needs not such costly gifts, my lord, to cause my old age, after much labor, to rest as softly and as gently in your grace as in silk and down.

[*Murmurs of applause.*

IVAR KOLLBEJNSON.

Never sat so open-handed a king upon the throne of Norway.

ALL.

Never.

IVAR KOLLBEJNSON.

What, to him, was Håkon Adelstejnsfostre?

OTHERS.

Or Magnus the Good ?

STILL OTHERS [*together*].

Or Olaf Kyrre, or —   [*General confusion.*

HALLKELL [*louder*].

There is not one of us here, who does not owe to him the half of his possessions.

IVAR KOLLBEJNSON [*still louder*].

Most of us owe him all!

GYRD.

The king is about to rise!

[*All spring to their feet; the king is assisted to rise. Some of the men come forward and group themselves about the king. In the mean while the tables are carried away.*

THE KING.

Before I became king, I could stand well upon my feet.

ALL.

Ha, ha, ha!

IVAR KOLLBEJNSON.

You were the swiftest runner that the North has ever seen.

HALLKELL.

I was there, my lord, when you deigned to race with Magnus's Gothic horse.

SEVERAL VOICES.

I too.   The king won three times.

THE KING.

But since I have been king, my strength has gone from my legs up into my head.

SEVERAL VOICES.

Ha, ha, ha! It has gone from his legs up into his head!

HALLKELL.

Yet I think that no man can now show the match to your legs, from ankles up to thighs.

IVAR KOLLBEJNSON.

A man who had the honor to feel of the royal legs once said that he should think them made at the forge were they not so white.

THE KING [*to Ivar Kollbejnson*].

Thou shalt feel of them.

IVAR.

Heaven defend me!

THE KING.

Why not?

IVAR.

To lay hands upon the king?

THE KING.

But I grant it.

IVAR.

For nothing in the world.

THE KING.

But I say thou shalt.

IVAR.

Such condescension! [*Feels.*] Yes, is it not — is it not like — all the way up!

THE KING.

Perhaps there are others here who would like to feel of my legs.   [*Several press forward.*

KOLL.

I think I have felt others as firm.

THE KING.

Hast thou, Koll?

KOLL.

Yes, of marble and gold.

THE KING.

Marble and gold.   Ha, ha, ha!

TJOSTULV.

It is most wonderful.   True horse-legs.   That is, I mean the fore-legs of a horse.   That is, I do not exactly mean a horse, but if a man were to have legs as strong as the fore-legs of a horse, I mean — yes, it is wonderful.
                                   [*Several feel of them.*

IVAR KOLLBEJNSON.

I could wish for nothing else upon earth, if I had such legs.

GYRD.

Yon man, who calls himself your brother, has waited without for three hours.

THE KING.

Bid him come to-morrow. Say that we have business.

IVAR INGEMUNDSON.

He has had that answer for eight days.

KOLL.

If I may say so, it may not perhaps be best to dismiss him too often.

HALLKELL.

Yes, let us have done with him once and for all.

THE KING.

I have thought — my men might have rid me of him — without me.

TJOSTULV.

Thus stood you once at the door of Sigurd Jorsalfarer; and he took you in and called you brother.

HALLKELL.

The difference is that Harald was the king's brother, and no one knows who this man is.

TJOSTULV.

Harald was put to the ordeal, and this man might crave as much.

HALLKELL.

The king cannot grant the right of ordeal to every stranger who comes with shameless demands to the court.

GYRD.

For we all know how the ordeal is managed.

KOLL.

If we all know it, we do not speak of it.

IVAR KOLLBEJNSON.

Tjostulv, speak further!

TJOSTULV.

Lord king, you have never yet allowed your predecessors to surpass you in gracious condescension. Do not so this day!

THE KING.

Tjostulv is right. What Sigurd Jorsalfarer did to me ought I to do to this chieftain. Lead him in!

[*Ivar Kollbejnson leaves.*

SIGURD STALLAR [*inclining*].

Will you not mount the throne?

THE KING.

Yes; he has been in Provence, in Rome, in Jerusalem, and in Micklegarth. We must show him that we know what is befitting our state.

KOLL.

But, my lord, perchance you show him too much consideration.

HALLKELL.

We know not yet who he is.

THE KING.

Well, we will remain here.   Thus ?

GYRD.

The king perhaps should sit, while the others stand.

THE KING.

Well, I will sit, and you shall stand.

TJOSTULV.

Were it not better that we should sit around upon the floor?   It is the custom with many foreign princes.

THE KING.

I will have that by no means. You shall not sit upon the floor.   [*They group themselves.*

SCENE SECOND.

The same. SIGURD, IVAR KOLLBEJNSON, *who stands a little aside.*

SIGURD [*on his knees before the king*].

May the blessed Olaf, our heavenly friend, be with us to-day at this meeting.   [*Rises.*

TJOSTULV.

This man looks as if he had suffered much.

IVAR.

Yes, yes.

SIGURD.

Lord king and brother, you have made me wait long.

Have now patience with me, hear me, and remember that a single hour to-day is to decide a conflict of fifteen years!

Magnus Barfod, your father, was mine also. Chieftain Koll Sæbjörnson was present in Stavanger church, when my mother revealed to me the fact before God's face. I was then twenty years old.

The mighty lord Sigurd Jorsalfarer, your brother, sat upon the throne of Norway. He was a natural son, as I myself, and I had the right to share his throne. But Koll Sæbjörnson and my mother convinced me that an unknown youth could not succeed in pressing such a claim. I did not feel in myself the strength to remain at home shut out from my rights, and I set out upon crusade; I sought for might and honor in foreign lands.

But God cast my ship and my purpose upon Scotland's coast, and broke them in pieces. A soldier from such unhallowed motives He would not own.

I understood not the sign then, but took service where I was, and day followed day in discontent.

I heard presently that close at hand had been accomplished what I had fled from doing; in the Orkneys, Norway's old fief, two brothers fought for the power. I journeyed thither and took the part of him who was the weaker.

Victory was mine; but the thought — for whom hast thou conquered? — awoke new plans in my soul; could I not have the kingdom, I would have the fief, and I cast the two weak brothers aside.

Then God closed for me all the paths of ambition with a fearful warning; in terror I forsook my plans, and even my obligations, and sought refuge in his embrace, seeming to catch sight of the crown that shines for us all in eternity's dawn. I took the cross.

For eight years my life was a crusader's. Many a great and solemn hour it gave me upon sea and land, but peace it gave me not. For a man may not efface his thoughts like a footprint, and the glowing sun of Nörvasund could not burn up within me the memory of my home, of my birth, and of the duties I had fled.

For it was indeed thus; I had fled them, not fulfilled them.

And in what company was I fallen? Monks, who sang before the battle, and preached of a glorious death, and fled in terror at the sight of an oriental turban through the palm-trees; knights, who embraced one another with brotherly kisses before the fight, and after, slew one another in strife for the leadership. Should I not better serve my God, I asked, in turning homewards, and fulfilling the least obligations that there awaited me?

Twice I had gone awrong; I would not do so a third time, and so I let my thoughts ripen during eight years, — can you understand how long that is for one who yearns?

TJOSTULV [*to Ivar Ingemundson*].

This man has suffered greatly, and there is truth in his speech.

THE KING.

Of a truth, he is our brother.

KOLL.

Be not hasty.

SIGURD.

When I stood once more in Denmark, I heard that

the two for whose sake most I had come had sought refuge in the cloister. But I heard also that Sigurd Jorsalfarer was dead, and his son Magnus become king, but of half the kingdom only, while the other half was ruled by my own younger half-brother — by you, my lord! You had dared what I had shrunk from, and the man who in his time had counseled me against it, [*he points to Koll Sæbjörnson*] had counseled you to do it, and stood now, high in rank, at your side! And when I looked towards Orkney, I saw that his son had been tempted to do what I fled for fear of doing, for he had conquered Earl Paul's kingdom!

TJOSTULV.

I could not have borne that.

GYRD [*to Hallkell*].

A marvelous career!

SIGURD.

There was sorrow and strife in both lands: I would not add to them. For two years I sailed as a merchant to and fro in the North Sea, but during those years Earl Paul of Orkney was captured and slain. And during the same time young Magnus of Norway was imprisoned and — blinded.

THE KING.

It was not I that did it, — not I!

SIGURD.

That I know, and the silence of your followers tells me who it was that did it.

It was soon reported about that your heart was gentle, that you gladly shared your power, and gave every man his right. Then thought I, perchance he will give me mine — the hour is come! In peace and unprotected will I go to him, tell him who I am, and what I have suffered. Therefore, O king and brother, am I come to-day. Will you not acknowledge me, then say but a word, and, Saint Olaf is my witness, I will retire. But if you incline to me, I am so easily led that I, who am passionate and strong, will try to make myself better; and a gentle brother may win the kingdom for us both.

THE KING.

It shall be so ! Yes, yes —

HALLKELL [*who has pressed forward*].

Lord king !

SIGURD.

When I see you sitting in your royal seat, and the poorest man about you better treated than I, who am your brother, unbidden thoughts arise in me. Let them not take hold of me, lest all I have won this day be lost again.

THE KING.

Hallkell, Hallkell, — we must not be too hard.

SIGURD.

I have roamed far abroad both in deed and in thought. I have fought in more battles than all of these men together; nearly all the known world have I seen, and plans and great experience do I bring with me. And I have so great a desire for activity that I can hardly control it. May it all prove a blessing to my fatherland!

There are moments in our life, when good and evil hold watch alike together — this may be such for me! And there are moments too for whose sake our whole being has been shaped — if this were such for you! If you perchance were made king but that you might do this great deed — and then should fail to do it!

But you will not! You remember too well how you yourself came to Sigurd Jorsalfarer; you will show your gratitude for the great fortune God has given you, and let some share of it be mine.   [*Falls on his knees.*

THE KING [*rising, and much moved*].

Yes, yes, thou art my brother! I will do all that is good by thee!   [*Embraces and kisses him.*

HALLKELL, GYRD, SIGURD STALLAR, BEJNTEJN.

King, king!   [*Great confusion among the chieftains.*

THE KING.

You say yourselves, he is my brother! Koll, thou didst hear his mother, what said she?

KOLL.

She said he was Magnus Barfod's son.

THE KING.

You all can hear that; and I feel it, at once feel it to be true.

GYRD.

But so weighty a matter should not be decided off-hand.

HALLKELL.

And in affairs of state the heart has hardly the first claim.

IVAR INGEMUNDSON.

Justice, rather.

THE KING.

Yes, justice! And I will do by him as Sigurd did by me ; that is justice !

HALLKELL.

Sigurd Jorsalfarer gave you the right to prove your birth; more than that he did not grant. That you became lord over the kingdom of Norway, that you owe to your chieftains, who can claim to be called upon for counsel in a matter of such immense importance, and it grieves me that I should be the first to remind the king of this.

THE KING.

My chieftains! Dear friends all! Would you have all that I possess, then take it. But in such a matter, when my heart tells me it would be an ill thing not to do justice — that I shall not live long, that I feel — I know not how to say it — I know not your speech — but only be kind to me, for I have only kindly feelings towards you.

TJOSTULV.

I shall never forget, O king, how nobly you have spoken and felt this day.

Undoubtedly the first thing to be done in this case is

to ask : does any man doubt that this man is Magnus
Barfod's son ?

MOST OF THE CHIEFTAINS.

Yes !

TJOSTULV [*pauses a moment*].

Good ! The next thing, then, is to grant him the ordeal ; thus he may prove his birth ; such grant was
made Harald.

HALLKELL.

We know what comes of that, if a few skillings can
be raised for the priests.

KOLL.

I must repeat that such things should not be said.

HALLKELL.

I am too good a subject to hide them ; the glowing
iron must not become the way to Norway's throne.

TJOSTULV.

I have heard that Hallkell was witness what time the
king went that way. I have never yet heard a man
stand up and brand himself a cheat.

THE KING.

There, there, no quarrel, friends ! Marshal, have we
no gift for Tjostulv ?

THE MARSHAL.

The gifts which we —

HALLKELL.

King Harald and his men cheated no one; there were other proofs than the glowing iron at hand. But the proofs of Sigurd's cause are entirely lacking.

THE KING.

Now it is getting so complicated. Koll, what sayest thou?

KOLL.

I have never known or heard, lord king, of the man whose cause was in question being present at the trial.

THE KING.

True, true, that is a great mistake. Sigurd, go in to my apartments — chieftain, follow — no, a greater, marshal, follow him. Trust in me, I will soon give you an answer.   [*Sigurd bows and leaves.*

SCENE THIRD.

The same, except, at first, SIGURD SLEMBE *and* SIGURD STALLAR, *the latter of whom soon returns.*

THE KING.

Now I will sit down, and we will consider it carefully. Speak thou first, Tjostulv.

TJOSTULV.

If discussion shall precede the ordeal, so let us begin. [*To Ivar Ingemundson.*] Is his mother living?

IVAR.

She is in the cloister.

TJOSTULV.

With all the greater force does her testimony come to us, for she has forsaken the world, and it is to her own shame that she witnesses. Is further proof needed? His very face is proof; send for Vidkun Jonson of Bjarkö, send for the old men who followed Magnus upon his glorious expedition, and we shall hear.

GYRD.

Tjostulv speaks as if he wished for Sigurd's welfare rather than the king's.

TJOSTULV.

It is a poor friend who wishes for aught but justice. Should we fail to do it, Harald may thereby lose more than half the kingdom. God help him who should bring misfortune upon us.

GYRD, SIGURD STALLAR.

These are threats!

THE KING.

No, no, do not quarrel! Tjostulv is right, and my own feelings count for much. Be kind, Hallkell!

HALLKELL.

That have I always been, I think. Tjostulv was far away then, when I brought you with me to Norway, and to the presence of Sigurd Jorsalfarer. It cost more to befriend you then than now.

THE KING.

Yes, yes, Hallkell, thou wast the first.

HALLKELL.

If our reward is to be that we now get two masters, I cannot say that it is great.

TJOSTULV.

The country's welfare is of greater consequence than Hallkell's, and to do justice does not always mean to accomplish one's desires.

HALLKELL.

The chieftains can best look after the country's welfare. Let Koll speak, I do not understand his silence.

KOLL.

I cannot in any way support Hallkell.

THE KING.

Hear that!

KOLL.

But I must rather admit that Tjostulv is right. I have never doubted that Sigurd was Magnus Barfod's son.

THE KING.

You hear!

TJOSTULV.

What more do we want?

KOLL.

But I remember that in my own life there was a time when we had two and three rightful kings, and they brought civil strife into every part of the land. It was the saddest time that I ever lived through.

THE KING.

Now it is getting so complicated — what shall we do?
Speak out briefly!

KOLL.

It is all the worse that it cannot be briefly spoken.
But from the first I have urged delay. Time brings
counsel.

THE KING.

Well, then, we will put the matter off.

TJOSTULV.

But you promised him to decide it.

THE KING.

So I did. It is as complicated as the very devil.
Cannot we decide something?

TJOSTULV.

Yes; whether or not he is your brother, for example.

GYRD, SIGURD STALLAR, HALLKELL, BEJNTEJN.

No, to do that would be to decide all.

HALLKELL.

That is a trap.

THE KING.

What shall we do, then?

GYRD [*in a low voice, to the king*].

Do you not remember whom you promised to see
after the banquet?

THE KING.

Thunder and lightning, I forgot all about it!

GYRD [*whispering*].

You will be sorry if you make her wait.

THE KING.

She will make me pay for it, she will!

TJOSTULV.

Let this day be marked by a kingly deed. Decide the matter before you go.

THE KING.

But, my good man, I have done all that I can.

TJOSTULV.

Give him at least a few words of comfort; tell him that he may still hope.

THE KING.

Yes, he may hope; I will tell him that.

HALLKELL [*to Gyrd*].

He must not speak to him.

GYRD [*to the king*].

Cannot one of us tell Sigurd that?

THE KING.

Yes, that is better. Tell him, tell him, that he may hope.

TJOSTULV.

That is too little.

THE KING.

But my good man —

GYRD.

She is waiting.

THE KING.

Yes, yes !　　Oh ! how many things a king has to hear about — and do !

[*He goes, followed by the court, which has first formed in two ranks, and bowed to the king.*

SCENE FOURTH.

KOLL, HALLKELL [*in conversation at one side*] ; IVAR INGEMUNDSON, TJOSTULV [*on the other side*].　IVAR KOLLBEJNSON [*sits apart*].

IVAR INGEMUNDSON.

Lose not the king from sight these coming days. Perhaps all is not yet lost.

TJOSTULV.

The devil take the king, and Sigurd, and his cause !

IVAR INGEMUNDSON.

Do not say that !

TJOSTULV.

No, I will not say that either.　But I will go home to Viken.　I am weary of things here.

IVAR.

Do not that either.

TJOSTULV [*gloomily*].

Yes, I will. [*A pause.*] When the weather is fair and the sea calm, it is pleasant enough with such a king. But when the wind fills the sails so that a man can hardly hold the helm with his legs, our plight is a sad one.

IVAR.

Why did you support him?

TJOSTULV.

You must ask Koll: he thought for me.

KOLL [*crossing, while Hallkell leaves*].

Do you speak of me?

TJOSTULV.

Yes, we do. How can you stand before Harald and say that two kings are dangerous? Were you not the one who made Harald king at Magnus's side?

KOLL.

But we rid ourselves of Magnus as soon as possible.

TJOSTULV.

Was it in your thought to overthrow Magnus then?

KOLL.

Was the drunkard fit to be king?

TJOSTULV.

He was better than this — man of legs.

KOLL.

That is a matter of taste.

TJOSTULV.

At first I thought him merely lacking in speech, but 't is brains that he needs.

KOLL.

Who has ever said that a king need have brains ?
                    [*Tjostulv looks at him in wonderment.*

IVAR INGEMUNDSON.

God has said it.

KOLL.

Has he ? I did not know it. In any case, I do not think it wisely said.

IVAR INGEMUNDSON.

These are light words, and an old chieftain should know what Holy Writ says — and respect it.

KOLL.

My wise skald, I think you have read it awrong. For it is written that the king shall be the head, but not that he shall have one.   [*Ivar Ingemundson is silent.*

TJOSTULV.

Is it your honest thought that a king should be — what this one is ?

KOLL.

I will not set him up as a model. Yet he is a good man — that is, as long as good men are about him.

TJOSTULV.

So we have seen this day.

KOLL.

He did finely to-day, better than we expected. If such a man as Sigurd were to come to the throne or near it, all would be over with us.

TJOSTULV.

Then Sigurd's fault is that he has too good a head !

KOLL.

I am glad to see that you understand for once.

TJOSTULV.

What you say is shameful.

KOLL.

We know what we have ; we know not what we might get.

TJOSTULV.

And with this musty proverb you think to set aside a man's rights and the sufferings of a lifetime ! Think you that will bar the way for him, for his powers and the impulse that brings him to seek his father's throne ? If there come not a storm from this, I have had no skill to read those deep eyes that judged our meeting to-day.

KOLL.

The rights and the sufferings of one man do not weigh
with me against the fate of a people.   Whatever punish-
ment Koll Sæbjörnson may suffer for this faith, he will
endure with patience.   Good evening, friends!   [*Leaves.*

SCENE FIFTH.

TJOSTULV, IVAR INGEMUNDSON, IVAR KOLLBEJNSEN.

TJOSTULV.

You hear, Ivar, there is no escape. The proud heads,
raised above the masses, have only to signal each other,
and no one may enter their circle.

IVAR INGEMUNDSON.

A king must come some time who will strike down
many of them at one blow.

TJOSTULV.

What say you there?   The powerful chiefs, the
strength and the pride of the land?   God preserve us!

IVAR INGEMUNDSON.

Then is the world made for the few, and Christianity
a delusion.

TJOSTULV.

You quiet little man, you, what sort of ideas are these?

IVAR INGEMUNDSON.

Those that stir within half the world to-day.   Every

country seems to me like a closed vessel. Its cover is the kingly power, and the bands about it are the chieftains. But the noble wine is working, it will force up its cover, it will burst its bands, and flow in red streams over the blessed fields of Jerusalem. What is the crusader's song but the expression of that desire for freedom, that joy in active life, which breaks all bounds and loses itself in the infinite?

TJOSTULV.

If this be true, then is the whole world sick and draws its breath in pain.

IVAR INGEMUNDSON.

In the whole world there are only some ten thousand men who are free to work their will, to do which is for the soul what breath is for the body. The blood of southern lands is being spilt in the terrible crusade warfare, and thereby will they lose their power and come again to be led by the stronger. In northern lands these imprisoned forces will soon make their way over the jailers' bodies.

TJOSTULV.

You speak thus from your humble birth. Justice may still be had in the land, and there is a place for the strong: I have never seen things otherwise.

IVAR INGEMUNDSON.

Then you were not in Harald's court to-day.

TJOSTULV.

If it comes to that, Sigurd also will find that this is true.

IVAR INGEMUNDSON.

Then make it so! There are not many here who
know your strength, for you are yourself forgetful of it.
You are weary, because there is no more war, no high
aims, no oppressed cause to fight for. Take Sigurd's
cause upon your strong shoulders, and be once more
Tjostulv Åleson! You waste your life in this court.
For a moment you flash out and your noble heart is
stirred, but a question or a gift calms it again. Make
of these good impulses your daily thought, and it will
be with you as it ever is when a good man and a good
cause work together.

TJOSTULV.

Where is Sigurd?

IVAR INGEMUNDSON.

He waits in the king's apartments. But the king has
gone to his mistress, and there are now in all the land
but two men who think of Sigurd — you and I.

[*Tjostulv gives him his hand and leaves.*

IVAR INGEMUNDSON [*to Ivar Kollbejnson*].

Are you here?

IVAR KOLLBEJNSON.

Yes.

IVAR INGEMUNDSON.

Are you waiting for sombody?

IVAR KOLLBEJNSON.

Yes.

SCENE SIXTH.

SIGURD SLEMBE, TJOSTULV, IVAR INGEMUNDSON, IVAR KOLLBEJNSON.

SIGURD SLEMBE.

Is the king not here ?   Is there no answer for me ?

TJOSTULV.

No.

SIGURD.

Whither has the king gone ?

IVAR KOLLBEJNSON [*rising and coming forward*].

To his mistress.

SIGURD.

To his —   [*Pauses.*

IVAR KOLLBEJNSON.

Do you wonder ?

SIGURD.

I was prepared for everything else — but not for in- difference.

IVAR KOLLBEJNSON.

.When the fate of the imprisoned Magnus was to be settled — the king likewise went to his mistress.

SIGURD.

Is it possible !

IVAR KOLLBEJNSON.

When he asked about Magnus afterwards — they had cut off his foot, blinded him, and in still fouler fashion mutilated him.

SIGURD.

It was even so!

IVAR KOLLBEJNSON.

The chieftains thought that Bishop Rejnald of Stavanger had concealed Magnus's treasure. He would not confess, and so they hanged him out on the shore in all his priestly vestments; the king was drunk that day, and first learned of the deed next morning.

SIGURD.

And what did he then?

IVAR KOLLBEJNSON.

He went to church and got absolution.

SIGURD.

But what did he do with his chieftains?

IVAR KOLLBEJNSON.

He went hunting with them.

SIGURD.

What this man says, is it true?

TJOSTULV.

Ay, it is true. Ay, it is shameful, and something must be done.

IVAR KOLLBEJNSON.

There are more than you who say that.

SIGURD.

Who are you?

IVAR KOLLBEJNSON.

Chieftain here at court. But I was Sigurd Jorsal-farer's follower and his son's.

SIGURD.

What?   Are there men from Magnus's court here in Harald's?

IVAR KOLLBEJNSON.

More than half are of Magnus's old court.

SIGURD.

And you can eat Harald's bread?

IVAR KOLLBEJNSON.

We were waiting.

SIGURD.

For whom?

IVAR KOLLBEJNSON.

We heard that Sigurd Magnusson was cruising in the North Sea.   [*Sigurd springs forward, then pauses.*

TJOSTULV [*following him*].

No violence!

SIGURD.

You are right.

TJOSTULV.

Once in a perilous hour I broke my oath to the king. Since then I have never been quite myself. Do not overstep the limits of the law! But as far as they may stretch — and with all your great powers — and if you want help — [*Offers his hand.*

SIGURD [*taking it*].

Thanks.

IVAR KOLLBEJNSON.

I shall stand watch under your gallows within three days.

TJOSTULV.

Old man, thou dost not know us.

IVAR KOLLBEJNSON.

But I know Hallkell Huk and ten other leaders here at court. All depends upon acting the first.

SIGURD, TJOSTULV.

But how?

IVAR KOLLBEJNSON.

If you cannot guess, I will not say it. [*Silence.*

SIGURD.

Does more than half the court think with you?

IVAR KOLLBEJNSON.

They await but a signal.

TJOSTULV.

To-morrow I will have you all arrested, every man of
you, and charge you with plotting to murder the king.

IVAR KOLLBEJNSON.

To-morrow you will find something else to do, as certainly as that Koll and Hallkell were whispering here together just now.

SCENE SEVENTH.

The same. BEJNTEJN, *a Watchman.*

BEJNTEJN [*to Sigurd*].

In the king's name !   You are my prisoner !

TJOSTULV, SIGURD.

Prisoner !

BEJNTEJN.

You are charged with the murder of Torkel Fostre in
Orkney, and you are to be held prisoner until found
guiltless or doomed.

TJOSTULV.

Who gave this order ?

BEJNTEJN.

The king.

IVAR KOLLBEJNSON [*stepping up to Sigurd*].

. Now will you —   [*Points to his weapons.*

IVAR INGEMUNDSON [*approaching with outstretched hands from the other side*].

No !

SIGURD.

No !   So end my dreams !

[*He goes with Bejntejn and the watchman.*

ACT SECOND.

SCENE FIRST.

IVAR INGEMUNDSON.

*He is seated, and striking chords upon a harp, but soon stops, leans
upon it and speaks.*

Whence are these yearnings
That I cannot satisfy ;
And why have I sight,
When my eyes behold but sorrow ?

Look they out upon the world,
Are all things dark to them, mist-enfolded :
Look they here about me,
They are dimmed with pity.

For I see a people without a leader,
I see a leader without a people.
Oh, how the people suffer !
And the leader, how he yearns for them !

Knew the men, but knew they
That he were among them !
They behold but a man in chains,
And let him lie there.

The ship is torn asunder in the storm,
A fool at the helm : who can save her ?
He, he who lies beneath the deck,
Half dead and in chains.   [*Rises.*

Hear how they shriek
And stretch their arms toward thee !
They have safety with them,
And thou wilt not tell them !

Shall they all come to grief,
Because one is lacking ?
Wilt thou not offer up the fool,
That the many may live ?

Make clear to me : the Word says :
One shall suffer for many.
But many suffer for one,
Oh, make clear to me !

The wisdom thou gavest me
Confronts me with riddles,
And the light thou didst kindle
Leads me into darkness.

And not me alone,
But millions upon millions ;
Space has not room for the questions
Which earth sends up to heaven.

The weak pray in the cloister,
But the strong fare forth ;
They press one upon another,
And the land will not contain them.

Whither turn they?   Night veils their eyes.
"There is light in Nazareth!" cries one,
A hundred thousand echo the cry;
All men see it: "To Nazareth!"

But half die of hunger upon the way,
The other half fall by the hand of the heathen,
And pilgrims by the plague in Nazareth, —
Wert thou there, or wert thou not?

Oh, where art thou?
'The whole world is up
And seeks after thee,
And longs for thee!

Or wert thou in the famine?
Wert thou in the plague?
Wert thou in the sword of the heathen?
Dost thou preserve with the salt of wrath?
Dost thou make pure by the fire of suffering?
Dost thou see millions upon millions in thy future,
Whom thus thou wilt save?

Compared with them are the thousands who now
        suffer,
But as one;
And the one for whom I would pray,
As none!

I follow a slender stream
And come upon an ocean;
I look at a little drop,
And it dissolves in the infinite skies.

See how aimlessly I toss
Upon the waves of thought.
The wind has upset my little boat,
And I cling to the wreck.

Lead me, lead me,
No land is in sight!
Raise me, raise me,
I feel no bottom!

SCENE SECOND.

IVAR INGEMUNDSON, TJOSTULV ÅLESON, KOLL SÆ-
BJÖRNSON.   *A Page.*

TJOSTULV [*enters in haste; the page has just come from the king*].
Announce me to the king! Is some one there already?

THE PAGE.
Hallkell has just come.

TJOSTULV.
Hasten!   .[*The page starts to go.*

KOLL SÆBJÖRNSON [*entering in haste*].
Hold!   Announce me too!   [*The page goes.*
          [*The two chiefs greet each other in silence.*

KOLL SÆBJÖRNSON.
You are seated at the harp?

IVAR INGEMUNDSON.
Yes.

KOLL.

A song to the morning-star?

IVAR INGEMUNDSON.

Which is setting: yes.

KOLL.

At daylight, Ivar Ingemundson: it sets at daylight.

THE PAGE.

Chieftain Koll Sæbjörnson has audience!
[*Leaves. Tjostulv makes a movement of impatience.*

KOLL [*to Tjostulv*].

You may go before me when you are older than I.

SCENE THIRD.

TJOSTULV, IVAR INGEMUNDSON.

IVAR.

Tjostulv, why do you not speak to me? I need you.

TJOSTULV.

Silence is safe.

IVAR.

I see that you are working restlessly, tell me but this: ·
hope you for success?

TJOSTULV.

You can see for yourself in a brief half hour. Have
you been to his prison?

IVAR.

Yes. He is greatly changed; he is sterner, colder.
I will tell you, you should have Ivar Kollbejnson and
half the court arrested. Ivar is with him every day.
A dark dungeon is a fit place for evil designs.

TJOSTULV [*after a little thought, taking his arm*].

Have you seen the long ships that came to the wharf
to-day?

IVAR.

They are your own.

TJOSTULV.

I have undertaken an honorable mission to Tröndelag.

IVAR.

Will you forsake him, then?

TJOSTULV.

Know you who goes with me?

IVAR.

No.

TJOSTULV [*whispering*].

Sigurd : — hush !

IVAR.

Tjostulv, thus you will break the law !

TJOSTULV.

The law is with me. Still another comes on board.

IVAR.

The king ?

TJOSTULV.

The king himself!

IVAR.

Saint Olaf! How have you brought that about ?

TJOSTULV.

I had an idea. I have let the king promise every-thing to everybody, but at the same time he has promised me to free himself from his tormentors, and exchange ten masters for one.

IVAR.

Then Sigurd shall reign with him ? [*Tjostulv nods and makes a signal of caution.*] You have won many victories, war-tried chieftain, but none fairer or greater than this, or of such tremendous import.

TJOSTULV.

I almost think so myself; at least I am as happy as a child. But those two are speaking with the king alone. They may frighten him at the last moment; they may lead him to betray himself. If I but had him on board my ship !

IVAR.

How I envy you your gift of fitting the deed to the word !

TJOSTULV.

Icelander ! Come with us to Nidaros ! Hear Sigurd speak at Frostathing !

IVAR.

Yes, yes!

TJOSTULV.

A fresh breeze comes even now from the mountains.

IVAR.

I will get my festal garments.

THE PAGE [*enters*].

The king sends word that he is ready, — that he waits for you! [*Goes.*

TJOSTULV [*to Ivar*].

He has kept his counsel.
[*Goes in to the king; Ivar departs hastily.*

SCENE FOURTH.

KOLL *and* HALLKELL [*coming from the king's apartment*].

HALLKELL.

He went in joyously.

KOLL.

And his joy will be doubled when he finds two estates added to his honorable mission.

HALLKELL.

Such good fortune and the festal preparations for the journey make him forgetful of Sigurd's cause. Tjostulv is vain and nowise deep.

KOLL.

But the other is a deep one. What a following he has already! And who can his tools be!

HALLKELL.

We need not think of that, if we can but convey himself to some safe place. It is not enough to send Tjostulv to Tröndelag. Sigurd must away from Bergen, — far away.

KOLL.

I will have nought to do with that.

HALLKELL.

It is of more importance than the other. So long as Sigurd is here, no one is secure. I wake in terror every morning; I will put an end to that.

KOLL.

You have much courage, Hallkell.

HALLKELL.

Bejntejn has taken all upon himself; he is now on his way.

KOLL.

Well, I like it better so.

HALLKELL.

Wherefore?

KOLL.

It is good for a party to have such tools; one need not do the work himself.

HALLKELL.

I hold myself ready to answer for it at any moment.

KOLL.

That is as if you were to wear both Bejntejn's cloak and your own.

HALLKELL.

When Sigurd's disappearance shall become known, Bejntejn must be able to fall back upon us to save himself.

KOLL.

Who speaks here of us? I have given counsel against it from the start.

HALLKELL.

And yet you do not disapprove of it.

KOLL.

That is another matter. You ask me if I wish a dangerous man put out of the way, and I answer yes. But if you ask that you or I shall do the deed, I answer no.

HALLKELL.

You almost put me at my wit's end. I see that we cannot count upon your powerful help.

KOLL.

Does it seem so? When the matter becomes known, who can so well come forward and defend you as an impartial man?

HALLKELL.

You think of doing that?

KOLL.

So let me keep out of it. I know nothing of the matter, and my counsel is against your course.

HALLKELL.

Now I understand. Before evening Sigurd shall be a dead man.

KOLL.

God forfend! not that, I mean it. You would break all the laws, and he is a defenseless man.

HALLKELL.

But a dangerous man, and more dangerous every day.

KOLL.

I rejoice in your love of country and of king. But take good heed, Hallkell!

HALLKELL.

What can I lose? The king will do naught.

KOLL.

You may be worsted in your conflict with Sigurd, and the more closely you are entangled, the more severely will he punish you.

HALLKELL.

I have done far too much for him ever to forgive.

KOLL.

Your hair is thick and dark.   It would grieve me to
see it in the hands of the headsman.

HALLKELL.

Would you frighten me — or urge me on?

KOLL.

Your strife with Sigurd is for life and death.   Could
you yet spare him, it would be nobly done, Hallkell.

HALLKELL.

I will speak of it no more with you.

KOLL.

That is the wisest course.

HALLKELL.

Good — I will talk with Bejntejn.

KOLL [*indifferently*].

Bejntejn?

HALLKELL.

Bejntejn undertakes to convey him through the fjords,
but on the way —

KOLL.

It is a long way; farewell!

HALLKELL.

I will go with you.

KOLL.

You have to speak with Bejntejn.

HALLKELL.

He is outside.

KOLL.

Then I will stay here.

HALLKELL.

He can come in just as well.

KOLL.

My steps to-day should not fall in with yours or Bejntejn's.

HALLKELL.

Then I will go.   [*Goes.*

SCENE FIFTH.

KOLL, TJOSTULV.

KOLL [*alone*].

I must see how Tjostulv bears himself, whether he has the snare about his legs, or has slipped through it. Yet more joyful? It is about his legs, worthy man.

TJOSTULV.

See you aught strange about me?

KOLL.

Nothing at all.

TJOSTULV.

You look at me with so much compassion.

KOLL.

That is just because I see no change.

TJOSTULV.

I am still the same old fool, you mean?

KOLL.   .

Are you, indeed?

TJOSTULV.

And better be the same fool than the same knave.

KOLL.

You are at least quite as polite as ever.

TJOSTULV.

There is a politeness current here at court which I am tempted to test with the edge of a good sword. But it would be like hewing at wool.

KOLL.

You remind me of the boy who thought he might ford the river by putting on his father's shoes. What did you seek at court, Tjostulv?

TJOSTULV.

I saw that you were so well off here. But I see now that I should have waited until I was old; then one can better bend his back to pick up the crumbs from the master's table.

KOLL.

How was it, you got some honorable mission north-
wards ?

TJOSTULV.

Yes.

KOLL.

Your ships are at the wharf.   You took it, then ?

TJOSTULV.

It was the king's command.

KOLL.

And you also got to-day two choice farms for your
traveling expenses ?

TJOSTULV.

You are well informed.

KOLL.

So you have come to it also.

TJOSTULV.

Think you so ?

KOLL.

The crumbs are choice ones, but you must bend the
back to pick them up.

TJOSTULV.

Is it you whom I have to thank for the gift?

KOLL.

One would not think it from your speech to-day. But I am glad that you have taken them. And it would make me doubly glad could these gifts tell you who are indeed your truest friends, who in spite of everything best recognize the great services you have done for the king and for the upholding of the nation.

TJOSTULV.

These gifts were not needed to remind me of that. It has long weighed upon my soul, and has made me at last resolve that I would strive to make good the mistakes of my earlier years.

KOLL.

I must remind you also that the gifts have another meaning. They tell you, Tjostulv Åleson, who has the power here.

TJOSTULV.

And I must tell you something also. I have had word from many of the land's chieftains, from Vidkun of Bjarkö, from Gunnar of Gimse, from the best men of Tröndelag : they are weary of you, and they are ready with me to see Sigurd raised up at Harald's side.

KOLL.

What is this that you dare ?

TJOSTULV.

And I took the honorable mission just because it carries me thither, to those men, to Tröndelag, to the great rock of Frostathing, where Sigurd shall be chosen.

KOLL.

Tjostulv !

TJOSTULV.

For that I took the two farms also, for they will be of good use to me : Sigurd may gain many voices thereby in Tröndelag.

KOLL.

Rebel !

TJOSTULV.

For that too will I take Sigurd in my ship.

KOLL.

And you are rash enough to tell Koll Sæbjörnson all this !

TJOSTULV.

Ay, and cautious enough to add : the king goes with me — is now on board my ship. He sends you word that he would not pain you who have served him so long, that you and Hallkell and the other chieftains may stay here and watch over the empty stronghold. Farewell, old man ! *[Goes.*

SCENE SIXTH.

KOLL [*completely cast down*].

Just as I have led him into the straits he has got a pilot on board, and sets out for sea with full sails, — and the work of my lifetime goes with him ! Can nothing now be done ? Hallkell, Bejntejn, you come too late,

Sigurd is already on the king's ship. The king, the king, the king! To offer up his old faithful friends for an adventurer! Like all weak souls, he flies from those who mean well with him, and takes refuge with those who will cut short his days. For in a year he will have no shadow of power; the stronghold he dwelt in, guarded by strong men, will be overthrown; and the future of the land laid open to every storm!

What we built, then, was it so insecure that one man might in a moment overthrow it? Ah! I have often thought that the foundation on which we built was lawlessness, and that the higher our work was reared, the sooner it might fall.

What condition is less secure than that of the old depotism? When were we more utterly lawless than in the last days of Jorsalfarer's reign and the first days of his son's? We sought a refuge for ourselves and our laws, and we built it; now it is overthrown.

For Sigurd will bring back the old despotic rule. A man whom fifteen years of suffering have not made to forget his birth, he must feel assured of his calling; he will consult himself alone, he will overthrow our plans, and the land shall again tremble at one man's will. And after his death? It will remain as a timorous maiden, who awaits her wooer, and loses heart ere her prime.

The game is played out! The future shall remember of us only that we overthrew young Magnus, shall know naught of what we hoped to build, naught of our plan to surround this one sceptre with a mighty, hundred-towered stronghold. Now, Koll, the evening sun goes down, and sees not thy task accomplished.

SCENE SEVENTH.

HALLKELL, KOLL.

HALLKELL.

Up! rouse your people, chieftain; Sigurd's prison is wide open! I seek in vain for Bejntejn; perhaps he is seeking Sigurd.

KOLL.

Sigurd is in the king's ship, and the king goes with Tjostulv to Frostathing; there shall Sigurd be acclaimed. Ingratitude took from us our power, and foolishness will wreck it altogether. Lay out your ships: we will sail over to my son, and leave the land to its fate.

HALLKELL.

Shall we so! I will rather give Tjostulv battle in the midst of the fjord, and take the king from him.

KOLL.

Then would Hallkell Jonson be king of Norway, and the land worse off than before.

HALLKELL.

As long as the king is kept from his counselors he is an imprisoned man, and can only be king again when set free.

KOLL.

Such talk teaches me for the first time the uncertainty of the situation — that I deemed so secure.

HALLKELL.

What government upon earth can be secure, when the watchman leaves his post at the hour of danger?

KOLL.

That one for which I have done watchman's service has dismissed me. It hurts me, for I am old and have been faithful, but I will not raise arms against my own master and law, still less against my own work.

HALLKELL.

You spoke otherwise, Koll, when King Magnus was to be put out of the way.

KOLL.

Yes; then we sought to build up law and order upon a foundation of lawlessness: we see the consequences now.

HALLKELL.

You will not stay and stand by your friends?

KOLL.

I am too old to seek for a place under the new order; let them build, who can! I will go rest with my son.

HALLKELL.

Yes, we helped him to become earl of the Orkneys; you have got what you worked for, and now forsake us!

KOLL.

Your proud, unreasonable course has estranged the trust of king and people; and now, when all grows hollow about us, you fall upon your own friends.

HALLKELL.

Old hypocrite, I have spoken and acted when you feared to do so, and now you count it to be sin.

KOLL.

Feared? No, do not let men say that we were friends only when we shared in the danger.

HALLKELL.

Who is it that seeks to break the bonds between us?

KOLL.

I will do all for my friends, all but aid them in revolt against the supreme law.

HALLKELL.

Law? You speak of law? An hour since you spoke for Sigurd's death in defiance of all law. You are held fast in a web of contradiction. The spider of conscience watches from his corner, but you seek still to struggle with the wings of self-esteem!

KOLL.

We can cast down him who is dangerous to the supreme law, but we may not overthrow that law itself. If there be contradiction in this, my whole life has been at fault, and an eventide of regret awaits me.

HALLKELL.

Time for regret is always to be found, but not for action.   [*Starts to go.*

SCENE EIGHTH.

The same.   TJOSTULV, *later* IVAR INGEMUNDSON.

TJOSTULV.

Is Sigurd not here ?

HALLKELL *and* KOLL.

Is he not on your ship ?

TJOSTULV.

No ; I thought he might seek the king here, but the king is on board.

HALLKELL [*to Koll*].

Then Bejntejn was first, — and we are saved !

IVAR INGEMUNDSON [*enters*].

Is Sigurd not here ?

TJOSTULV.

No ; hast thou not seen him either ?

IVAR.

Yes, I have seen him.

TJOSTULV.

What dost thou mean ?   Where ?

IVAR.

When I went hence for my things, I could not bring myself to pass by his prison ; so I entered and told him

the king's men were coming for him ; that they would
take him to freedom, to you, to the king, to Nidaros, to
the throne ! He fell upon his knees, and burst out
weeping as he prayed. And I hastened home for my
things, and then back again to wait at his side. But the
door was open, and the watch said that the king's men
had come already — but Bejntejn was their leader !

TJOSTULV.

Bejntejn ! I am overmatched ! By you !

IVAR.

Yes, it is by them.

TJOSTULV.

The king's men are about to start for the ships. Stop
them here.   [*Ivar leaves.*

HALLKELL.

What shall they do here ?

KOLL.

You will not dare ! —

TJOSTULV.

Trustingly has he followed his murderers, for he
thought it the way to freedom, to me, to the king, to
Nidaros, to the throne — and they have led him to the
caves of death. Oh shameful baseness ! Oh accursed
law-breakers ! Oh robbers in a king's council ! Ay, in
the king's council, where your voices from the first day
have clamored for blood ! So this victim also must
follow King Harald's memory like a horrid spectre, even

as the mutilation of Magnus, as the murders of Bishop
Rejdar and the captured chieftains who suffered for
Magnus's sake! You have given him the name of king,
and have robbed him of the name of man through all
eternity! You have degraded him to an ambush for
your murderous lust! And who is he that you now
have murdered? The king's brother, the oldest son of
Magnus, and the greatest chieftain who has ever come
to Norway! He was the salvation of the kingdom; he
was the man we should have awaited when we cast in
our lot with Harald; he it was who might have made
good the wrong you did. And you have destroyed him,
have destroyed the country's hope! My work too have
you destroyed; after the strain of months, I grasped it
at last; I held my work up to the God of the future,
and it is broken in my hands!

HALLKELL.

You may well mourn now, Tjostulv, for your revolt is
ended with Sigurd. How does it stead you now to have
fooled your old friends, and enticed the king as prisoner
upon your ship, misled him into traitorous ways? Nay,
spare your angry looks; you are the law-breaker! We
are they who have saved the land! Its fate shall not
be cast upon the moods of an adventurer, but rest beneath the guard of sure men. You have seen how they
can strike to earth whoever withstands them.

[*In the meanwhile the approach of the king's men is heard.*

TJOSTULV.

No, your bloody rule is at an end. Like an evil hail-
storm you have shattered my plans, but yours shall no
more wax in the land!

KOLL.

You stand there with threats and speak like God Almighty. When the fit is over, you will see how small your strength has grown. The king's council is again in power, and you alone are shut out from it. Hallkell, let us go to the king!

TJOSTULV.

You shall never see his face more! The guards are here. [*The music stops.*] I am their captain; from this day I am second in the kingdom. In the king's name you are my prisoners, and shall be taken to the very dungeon in which Sigurd sat.

BOTH.

What dare you?

HALLKELL.

Think you of the outcome?

TJOSTULV.

I first do my duty, and think of the outcome afterwards.

HALLKELL.

None but the king can condemn us. We demand to be brought before the king!

KOLL.

Any one who will be is king now.

TJOSTULV.

Thus you reap the fruit of your own sowing.

SCENE NINTH.

The same. IVAR INGEMUNDSON, IVAR KOLLBEJNSON.

TJOSTULV.

Captain, take these men to the dungeon in which Sigurd sat.

IVAR KOLLBEJNSON.

Your weapons!   [*Koll gives up his.*

HALLKELL.

For five years it has been drawn only in the king's defense.   [*Gives his.*

TJOSTULV [*to Koll*].

Give us some jest, since you are about to leave the court; you had so many of them but now.

KOLL.

That I should go, and you stay, is jest enough.
                    [*They turn to go.*

IVAR KOLLBEJNSON [*in haste to Tjostulv*].

Gyrd is without.

TJOSTULV.

Him also, him also!   [*Ivar Kollbejnson opens the door.*

KOLL *and* HALLKELL [*just stepping out*].

Gyrd!

SCENE TENTH.

The same. GYRD.

GYRD.

A message from Bejntejn !

ALL.

From Bejntejn !

GYRD.

Bejntejn was to take Sigurd to a safe place ; he followed willingly. But he grew restless when he saw them turn in through the fjord. Soon he rose to his feet, but two men rose also and held him by the cloak. Then did Sigurd grasp them with either hand, dragged them over into the ice cold water with him, then freed himself, and swam away under the water. Before the boat could be turned about and the two men saved, he had reached the mountain's foot, and soon they saw him climbing up its slippery side with neither hat nor cloak.

HALLKELL.

Then the last rope is broken.

KOLL.

And we are plunged into civil war.

IVAR INGEMUNDSON.

Poor Sigurd ! In the icy fjord at dead of winter ; on the bare mountain without cloak or hat !

TJOSTULV.

Evil thoughts will rise up in him.

IVAR INGEMUNDSON.

Shall we send out the guards to lead him back?

TJOSTULV.

He will see a foe in every man who draws near, and flee from him, for never was man treated more treacherously.

GYRD.

Bejntejn called out to him that he should not be slain, but taken to a safe place, yet he still fled.

TJOSTULV.

His flight has saved you from a murder.

KOLL.

Common danger must unite us now. From this hour there is civil war. Our acts, by which we thought to quench the fire, will blow it up to a glowing heat in his wronged soul, and all the land will soon burn in it.

TJOSTULV.

Yes, should Sigurd live, you have kindled a great fire.

HALLKELL.

The weather is cold, and the wind from the north.

GYRD.

The nights are harsh in the mountains.

TJOSTULV.

But his spirit will not be quenched there.

KOLL.

No, he is stronger than other men.

IVAR INGEMUNDSON.

But the patience, the peaceful thoughts he brought back from fifteen years of exile, they will freeze to death this night.

GYRD.

Can we not stay his hand yet?

IVAR KOLLBEJNSON.

Can we not offer him what before was ready to be offered?

KOLL.

For my part, face to face with this danger, I would advise that we offer everything.

[*Hallkell and Gyrd converse together apart from the rest.*

IVAR INGEMUNDSON.

He will no longer have faith in you.

TJOSTULV.

Thou art right. The storm must come. When its last thunderous burst shall be over, who can say what trunks will be cleft, what dams burst open, whose fields and hearths laid waste by flood and avalanche!

IVAR KOLLBEJNSON [*with much feeling*].

You, Tjostulv, can master the whole danger. The

king is in your power, these others as well; a little pressure and everything will give way — there is no more strength to resist.

HALLKELL, GYRD, KOLL [*coming forward*].

No, no.

TJOSTULV.

No, there is something which is worse than civil war.

KOLL.

Then you will fight against Sigurd, Tjostulv?

TJOSTULV.

Against Sigurd?   No!

GYRD, HALLKELL.

Will you forsake the king?

TJOSTULV.

I forsake both.   You may fight who will; you all are free!

IVAR KOLLBEJNSON.

Tjostulv!

IVAR INGEMUNDSON.

And you yourself?

TJOSTULV.

I will go hence to my lands.

IVAR KOLLBEJNSON.

Tjostulv.

TJOSTULV.

My toil and my hopes are turned to child's play.

IVAR INGEMUNDSON.

None of us has won; we all have lost.

KOLL.

We have fought as in a mist, two divisions of the same army, and have only wounded one another.

TJOSTULV.

For that to be done was beyond our strength.

HALLKELL.

Let us go to the king, tell him of the land's danger, and offer him our help !

KOLL, GYRD.

Yes, to the king !

TJOSTULV.

I go with you to take my leave.

IVAR KOLLBEJNSON.

Tjostulv !   [*Tjostulv goes without responding to the call.*

IVAR INGEMUNDSON.

I will seek the church and let a mass be said for the soul who must wrestle with his God to-night up in the ice of the mountains.

[*He leaves, and Ivar Kollbejnson slowly follows.*

SCENE ELEVENTH.

A narrow mountain cavern.

It is dark, SIGURD *comes in from above on hands and knees.*

SIGURD.

Now they can row home with Sigurd's cloak and cap.
Some gray-white night when the north wind blows cold
I shall claim them both again. It is damp here. Nothing seems to live here. When I stand still, I freeze.
My wet clothes are stiff with ice and cut me. When I
walk, they rattle like some skeleton following in my footsteps. It is death himself! The grisly one would own
me, since I have swum his broad fjord. But life has
cheated me, and I will cheat death. The biting mountain snow cannot reach me down here, and my limbs
will give each other warmth. And so I will think upon
how it is that I am come hither.

First of all I am a king's son. But in my twentieth
year I was changed into a black dog and driven out into
the world. A madman sat in my father's seat; then
came a child, then a simpleton. But I was so chased
about that I grew tame and licked the hand that struck
me. Then came I home again, and the simpleton who
sat where I should sit was asked if he knew me. Yes,
said he, this is my changed brother: I will take him to
my embrace. But the embrace was that of the deep,
cold sea, which would swallow me up, and behold, I
sank not, I rose. But the dog's skin sank, and he who
rose was a king (*he rises*), armored in revenge, with
despairing eye, and a red, flaming sword. And when
the sword is wielded it shall flash over all Norway, and
tears shall follow as close as rain upon the lightning

flash; yet all the tears of the race could not suffice to relieve the weight now upon my heart.

[*He throws himself down; then half rises, leaning on his elbow.*

Shall I live and thus suffer ? Death is better — and death it was they would have given me, but I got life instead. Then it must be they who shall die, for we cannot all live.

When I endured the heat of Asia I said to myself: thy life must be worth something. If I endure this night, it must be that other lives are worthless.

A king ! What thoughts were not mine, when I thought of myself as a king ! In every land where I sojourned, I gathered a jewel for his crown, great men gave wisdom to his sway, all good laws were his. But when I came home to my throne, a toad had crept up into it. Shall I leave it there, and fare further myself ?

[*He rises higher and higher.*

No, by the righteous God, thus far and no further. From this time onward, it is I who will pursue, and they who shall seek for shelter. I will force the king's stronghold, and sharp as the winter wind shall be the reckoning. Yet more, I will cast these counsellors of dishonor out of the open windows, as of yore did Israel's avenger himself, and his council, and his servants, great as well as small, — all who have suffered injustice to be done. The unhappy shall be happy now; there shall be no more sobbing, even in the remotest corner — ah, I hear it even here, and most from a cloister in Nidar-holm. Magnus ! Plunged into the dreary night at eighteen years ! I will raise him up on velvet and re-store him to his friends. But every one who forsook him shall be cast out; every one who fought against him shall die ; all who shall defy us both shall die also, ay, were there ten thousand! Who is looking at me from that corner?

Can a man see himself? Fever from the chill waters. For if I see myself for the first time to-day, who was I yesterday?

Revelation is granted to the race, but the individual gets only that which he may find in his fortunes and in his own heart. That after fifteen years of exile I should be brought hither; I may call that a revelation.

The ice of this night is for the sharpening of my will. The droppings of a thousand years have hollowed out this refuge for one night's use.

There again! Speak, if thou art more than mine own fancy! Or take one step towards me, that I may know thou art here. Thou dost!

They say that only he who is about to die sees himself. Shall I die, then? For I surely see myself; now I lift my hand, now let it fall. I am ill; I must find some one to save me. I am freezing; I will sit down; see — he too sits down in a corner. How I shiver, and yet my head is burning, burning with a hundred thousand fires. What if I were to die? Why did I not perish in the water? Why did they not kill me? No, I shall not die, but I shall suffer. If only the day would come, that I might find my way to shelter!

ACT THIRD.

The king's bridge at Bergen, the fjord beneath, but so far down that an approaching boat cannot be seen. Rocks upon the side stretching out to the fjord. Night, near Christmas time.

SCENE FIRST.

A WATCHMAN, A NUN.

The watchman sits on a rock in the background; the nun on the other side in the foreground; she tells her beads, bowing down; pauses at times, and looks out upon the fjord.

THE WATCHMAN [*singing* "Magnus is blinded"].

" But once more let me the heavens see,
   When the stars their watch are keeping,"
Young Magnus begged, and fell on his knee,
It was sad to see,
And the women away turned weeping.

"Let me once more the mountains see,
   And the blue of the ocean far-reaching,
Only once more, and then let it be ! "
And he fell on his knee,
While his friends were for pity beseeching.

" Let me go to the church that the sacred sight
   Of the blood of God may avail me;
That my eyes may bathe in its holy light,
Ere the day take flight,
And my vision forever shall fail me ! "

But the sharp steel sped, and the shadows fell,
As the darkness the day o'erpowers.
" Magnus our king, farewell, farewell ! "
" So farewell, farewell,
    All my friends of so many glad hours."

SCENE SECOND.

The same. IVAR INGEMUNDSON. *The watchman rises.*

IVAR [*approaching him*].
God's peace upon your watch !   The night is cold.

THE WATCHMAN.
A cold night.

IVAR.
The moon is full and the sea calm.

THE WATCHMAN.
Calm sea.

IVAR.
It is dismal to watch alone.

THE WATCHMAN.
I am not alone.

IVAR.
No, I see now, — a woman.

THE WATCHMAN.
She is crazy.

IVAR.

No cheerful company in the dark.

THE WATCHMAN.

No; this is the third night she has come.

IVAR.

You must speak to her.

THE WATCHMAN.

She does not answer.

IVAR.

What does she all night long?

THE WATCHMAN.

Sits there, as you see.

IVAR.

Does no one here know her?

THE WATCHMAN.

She does not belong hereabouts.

IVAR.

You ought to try and get her under shelter, she will freeze to death.

THE WATCHMAN.

Yes, but she will not go.

IVAR [*to the nun*].

God's peace!

THE WATCHMAN.

Let him try it!

[*Crosses over. The nun looks up, then bows her head, and prays as before.*

IVAR.

You must be freezing, worthy sister — sitting there so quietly. [*The nun nods and continues as before.*] Will you seek shelter? [*The nun nods.*] Is it to do penance that you sit thus here at night? [*The nun raises her head, looks out to sea, then lets it sink again.*] Jesus, I thought so: it is she! Tora! [*The nun makes a motion as if frightened.*] Do you not know me any more? [*The nun looks at him long, then shakes her head.*] Ivar, who sought you out in the cloister? Who spoke of your son?

THE NUN [*rising*].

My son — where is he?

THE WATCHMAN.

She answers him!   [*Goes back and forth by the fjord.*

THE NUN.

Tell me, but softly. They would slay him.

IVAR.

I cannot tell you.

THE NUN.

Is there no one here who can tell me?

IVAR.

No one, I think — but God.

THE NUN.

Dead — mean you? — No, he is not dead.

IVAR.

Would you mourn if you knew it to be so?

THE NUN.

No, — for then no one could harm him any more.

IVAR.

Then be glad, for he is dead.

THE NUN.

Have you seen his body?

IVAR.

He died in the mountains. He cannot be found till spring, when the snow melts.

THE NUN.

No, he is not dead in the mountains.

IVAR.

Were he alive, we should have heard from him by this. Tjostulv Åleson has had search made in every hut about the mountain to which he escaped; he has also asked in the seaports, but Sigurd has come to none of them. Believe me, I spoke with Tjostulv but yesterday.

THE NUN.

He is not dead; he comes to me in my dreams every night. He is pale; he suffers, suffers.

IVAR.

You may be at rest.   It is well with him where he is,
and he awaits you.

THE NUN.

Here, here he awaits me.   [*Pause.*

IVAR.

You are ill, Tora.

THE NUN.

But I must stay till he comes.

IVAR.

From whence ?

THE NUN.

He shall rise up from the sea.

IVAR.

From the sea ?

THE NUN.

I will tell you, but do not repeat it to any one; he
will rise up from the sea and look about him. Peace
has taken flight from him, he is pursued by hate, he will
ever on, ever on — but he must come to me. I have not
seen him for fifteen years, but I have waited for him
every hour of all those years.

IVAR.

Have you leave from the cloister to go thus about the
land ?

TORA.

No; you must not tell where I am.

IVAR.

And you journey in search of him?

TORA.

Ever. Ah, they will capture him at last, and blind him as they did Magnus.

IVAR.

His eyes are closed to this world. Come, Sigurd was dear to me, I could do naught for him, let me do what I may for his mother.

TORA.

My son is dear to you?

IVAR.

Yes.

TORA.

How looks he now? Pale, is he not?

IVAR.

Pale.

TORA.

And with the high forehead?

IVAR.

With the high forehead. But his hair is thin.

TORA.

It was always like silk. Such hair soon falls.

IVAR.

Come home with me and I will tell you more of him,
how fair he is still, and what he said.

TORA.

Yes, I will come, when it is morning.

IVAR.

But it is morning already.

TORA.

No, I can tell the time by my prayers. Thanks, many
thanks !   [*Bows and sits down.*

IVAR.

Look at the watchman, how he freezes. Think you
that you can bear more than he? Should you shorten
your own life? Should you take the days from God?

TORA.

Do you think I am doing that?

IVAR.

Yes, I think so.

TORA [*rises*].

Well, then. Well, I should not do that. But I am
not very cold.

IVAR.

Because you are so ill that you do not feel it.

TORA.

Is it so? But if my son should come just when I have gone?

IVAR.

You speak like one who is ill, too. What would you of him?

TORA.

Hist! Is there no one who can hear us?

IVAR.

No.

TORA.

I would say to him, that for Christ's dear blood's sake he must put an end to all this.

IVAR.

Come now.

TORA [*pleadingly*].

Do you not think I can sit out this one night?

IVAR.

It may become eternity's night for you.

TORA.

So? Oh, then, I must go with you.

IVAR.

Here is my mantle, wrap it well about you. How you are chilled!

TORA.

Yes, — but I —

IVAR.

Lean on my arm.

TORA.

Thanks, many thanks !　But I —

IVAR.

No, this way.

TORA.

Oh no, I cannot !　[*Falls on her knees.*]　If he were to come just now !

IVAR.

The dead rise not up from the sea.

TORA.

He is not dead !

IVAR.

If he live, I will find him for you.

TORA.

What say you ?

IVAR.

Wherever he may be in the world, I will bring you together.

TORA.

You promise me that upon the cross of Christ ?

IVAR.

Yes.   [*She rises with his help.*

TORA.

Then I will go with you.

IVAR.

The day will soon be here ; the stars are fading.

THE WATCHMAN [*seawards*].

Hold, who is there ?

TORA.

The oar-strokes from a boat !

VOICE FROM THE SEA.

Captain !

IVAR.

It is the one who looks after the watch.

TORA.

But there are many.

IVAR.

His rowers.   Come now.   [*They go.*

SCENE THIRD.

THE WATCHMAN, IVAR KOLLBEJNSON, *followed by* SI-
GURD SLEMBE, ERLEND, *and two others.*

IVAR KOLLBEJNSON.

Do you push the boat off ?

SIGURD SLEMBE.

We need it no longer.

IVAR [*softly to the watchman*].

Is the king in town to-night?

THE WATCHMAN [*softly*].

Yes.   [*Laughs.*

IVAR [*laughs*].

Did any one go with him?

THE WATCHMAN.

A page.   [*Passes over.*

IVAR [*to Sigurd and the others*].

He sleeps with his mistress.

ERLEND [*to Sigurd*].

Lord! Shall we wake him, then?

SIGURD.

What art thou thinking of?

ERLEND.

If we slay him in sin, he will go to hell.

IVAR KOLLBEJNSON.

When Sigurd is king, he can have masses said.

ERLEND.

One does not kill even a beast in his sleep.

SIGURD.

Death comes easiest in sleep.

ERLEND.

Let him say a short pater noster.

IVAR.

With three swords in his face he will not think of that.

ERLEND [*pointing to Sigurd*].

The brother can help him. He has had priestly training.

SIGURD.

Hear! The cock crows the second time : it is the hour !   [*They go.*

SCENE FOURTH.

THE WATCHMAN [*sits down where the nun sat*].

I wonder, will the little one let mother rest to-night. If he but turns in his sleep, she awakes. A mother is a strange thing. If children only knew what she does for them when they are little, they would be more thoughtful when they are grown.

But who can think of everything? I think it is not worth while to think. What must happen happens, and crazily enough, for the most part, but we cannot help it. Sin came into the world by —   [*Sings.*

> Sin and Death, at break of day,
> Day, day,
> Spoke together with bated breath ;

Marry thee, sister, that I may stay,
Stay, stay,
In thy house, quoth Death.

Death laughed aloud when Sin was wed,
Wed, wed,
And danced on the bridal day ;
But bore that night from the bridal bed,
Bed, bed,
The groom in a shroud away.

Death came to her sister at break of day,
Day, day,
And Sin drew a weary breath :
He whom thou lovest is mine for aye,
Aye, aye,
Mine he is, quoth Death.

A WOMAN'S VOICE [*in the distance*].

Help, help!   The king is slain, the king !

THE WATCHMAN [*falling on his knees*].

Saint Olaf, where art thou ?   Pater noster, noster pater,
pater, pater, pater, pater, I cannot think —   Thanks
for the meat and drink which thou in fit time hast set
before us, so that we were all filled ; the poor —

THE VOICE [*nearer*].

Help, help!   The king is slain, the king !

THE WATCHMAN [*on his feet*].

Help, help!   The king is slain, the king !   I must
pass it on, though it burn my tongue.   God save the

king, and give peace to the land, and good seasons, fish from the sea and bread from the dry earth, no pestilence fall upon people —

A MAN FROM THE OTHER SIDE.

Up, up! All the king's men!   [*Horns are heard.*

THE WATCHMAN.

Up, up! All the king's men! I ought to have shouted that before.

SCENE FIFTH.

THE WATCHMAN [*several others enter*].

HALLKELL HUK [*half-dressed, sword in hand*].

Whence is the cry?

.

THE WATCHMAN.

From yonder! Now it comes from yonder too! Saint Olaf, to whom does the great dog belong?

HALLKELL.

I see no dog.   [*Running.*

BEJNTEJN [*enters*].

Yonder?

THE WATCHMAN.

Yes, the chieftain Hallkell Húk ran yonder, but the great black dog came from this side, and the captain came from the sea. [*Bejntejn sets out running, several*

others cross the scene partly clothed.] Now they are all
running as if they had hot coals in their shoes, and now
they leave me here alone. Sigurd Jorsalfarer has been
seen here before, sword in hand, they say, and to-night
his son Magnus has brought him out again. No watchman can stand this. God save the king ! It was to-
day — therefore —   [*Seeks to make his escape.*

KOLL [*meets him*].

Dost thou hold the watch here ?

THE WATCHMAN.

No, I must be excused from that.

KOLL.

Art thou dismissed ?

THE WATCHMAN.

If I am not dismissed now, I never will be ! [*Runs off.*

KOLL.

With the king falls the law, and with the law obedience. [*Hallkell returns.*] Hallkell, is it true ?

HALLKELL.

I have seen him myself. Five thrusts through the
breast.

KOLL.

And the murderer ?

HALLKELL.

It was dark, no one could see him. Who thinkest
thou ?

KOLL.

The same as thou.

HALLKELL.

Have I named any one?

KOLL.

I see it in your terror.

HALLKELL.

Yes, Sigurd is alive; this was the first word from him.

KOLL.

And the king was guiltless, Hallkell!

HALLKELL.

Koll, we have slain the king, we, we!
                    [*He sits down and hides his face in his hands.*

KOLL.

Speak not of that, but of what shall now be done.

HALLKELL.

An invisible hand is against us. Every arrow we shoot comes back into our camp.

KOLL.

What shall we do?

HALLKELL.

Nothing steads us! We are entrenched within strong defenses, yet death climbs over the walls at night and slays the king in his sleep.

KOLL.

Dost thou lose courage, Hallkell?

HALLKELL.

Soon will he come noiselessly to thee, to me, to all the king's friends; for there are traitors among us, and the people desert our cause.

KOLL.

Shall we sit down, then, and wait for death?

HALLKELL.

Whom shall we rise up and fight for?

KOLL.

For what we have always fought for.

HALLKELL.

I am not merely a sword to be plucked from the hand of the slain. All that I could fight for lies low with him.

KOLL.

A man alone has fallen, but a cause remains — and trust me, — Sigurd has set it on its feet.

HALLKELL.

There is no being of flesh and blood to whom thou givest an hour's thought, except to think of how thou canst make use of him.

KOLL.

When we get time we can talk about the king. Hear me: had Sigurd met him in open strife, God knows what might have come of it. But he murdered him, and has turned the whole people against him, and united the powerful in one common fear and bitterness of feeling.

[*Alarm bells are heard; also, in the distance, uproar and the sound of drums.*

HALLKELL.

With what purpose ? We have no more a king.

KOLL.

Hast thou lost thy wits, or forgotten Saint Olaf's law ? His children !

HALLKELL.

Boys of four years and less.

KOLL.

Had we taken a child the first time instead of a simpleton, we should hear no alarm bells now. But with them there comes to me a powerful voice : Save the land, it calls, it is for you that Sigurd has toiled this night. During the period of regency we may strengthen the chieftain power which we have created, and build up a peaceful future for the land.

HALLKELL.

They are the old ideas that you thus trifle with on the night of the king's death.

KOLL.

Trifle ? No ! With new force they seize upon his empty crown and offer it to us ; they raise up his bloody purple in the midst of the tumult, as a holy standard to protect us ; they bring his fatherless children before the tearful people, to be acclaimed by them with blows upon their shields. Can you not see that, Hallkell?

HALLKELL.

I see what you forget — the people's warrior, their idol —

KOLL.

Tjostulv!

HALLKELL.

He is released from his oath now. Whither he goes the people will follow.

KOLL [*affrighted*].

You are right! Sigurd had Tjostulv in mind when he did this.

HALLKELL.

And what if Tjostulv should give fealty to Sigurd?

KOLL.

Tjostulv acts like a drowsy man. Perhaps he will declare for neither side.

HALLKELL.

The people will crowd about him and awaken him.

KOLL.

Much depends upon this moment. The dam is burst and the flood rushes by. We do not yet know where to find the fords.

HALLKELL.

Or where the water is most shallow.

KOLL.

A single stone in the path is often enough.

HALLKELL.

Let us see! A great crowd comes from the town. Their weapons gleam in the sun's first rays. It is the new day of strife that now begins.

KOLL.

Are they Sigurd's men or ours?

HALLKELL.

Either's, as it may chance. Let us step aside. I am ill at ease in a crowd.

KOLL.

No, no, if the stream is loose, let us go with the current; some hindrance may arise which will be useful to us.

[*The people draw nearer in a tumult, speaking hurriedly together; the following scene passes quickly.*

SCENE SIXTH.

The same. THE PEOPLE, *headed by* IVAR KOLLBEJNSON.

SEVERAL VOICES.

We would have peace in the land!

OTHERS.

We will not have strife!

SEVERAL.

Peace and trade!

OTHERS.

Down with them who stir up strife and murder !

SEVERAL.

Down with the chieftains !

ALL.

Down with them !

SEVERAL.

There are two of them !

OTHERS.

Did they kill the king ?

ALL.

Murderers !

IVAR KOLLBEJNSON [*in disguise*].

No, no ! These were the king's friends ! Know you
not Koll and Hallkell ?

SEVERAL.

Are those the bloodhounds ?

OTHERS.

Those who put out Magnus's eyes ?
                    [*Shouts of abuse and general tumult.*

A CRONE [*with shrill voice*].

Out upon you, bloodsuckers !

IVAR KOLLBEJNSON.

Here comes Tjostulv Åleson.

SCENE SEVENTH.

The same. TJOSTULV ÅLESON [*cast down*].

SEVERAL.

Hurrah for Tjostulv Åleson !

ALL.

Hurrah !

SEVERAL.

Help the people to have peace !

OTHERS.

Help us against the chieftains !

THE CRONE.

Put their eyes out, the —

TJOSTULV [*reluctantly speaking*].

Let me be !

SEVERAL [*seizing her*].

Let him be !

THE CRONE.

Ah !

KOLL [*to Tjostulv*].

What think you of this ? ·   [*Tjostulv does not reply.*

ALL.

We will help whom you help !
> [*They all promise one after the other.*

IVAR KOLLBEJNSON [*with meaning*].

There lives no longer any king to whom you owe allegiance.

THE PEOPLE.

Name him to whom thou wilt submit!

IVAR KOLLBEJNSON.

Name also them who stand in thy way.

ALL.

Name them!

KOLL.

Do not listen to that, Tjostulv!

IVAR KOLLBEJNSON.

They stand in the way! [*Pointing to Hallkell and Koll.*] They betray themselves!

ALL.

Yes, they!   [*The people approach threatening.*

HALLKELL [*his hand on his sword*].

Back! Your throats roar lawlessness; pretend not to invoke the law against us, for you yourselves rend it and trample it under foot!

IVAR KOLLBEJNSON.

Lay hands upon them! Down with them! All the bells of vengeance now ring!

          [*They are surrounded; great uproar.*

HALLKELL.

Tjostulv! The horrors of this night will be on your head!

KOLL.

Speak to them!

TJOSTULV.

Quiet, good people, quiet! . Who is he that hath slain the king?

KOLL.

He bides in the night whence he came forth!

HALLKELL [*while the crowd still menaces him*].

Yes, it is one man's hate which has loosed all the evil spirits this night! Mark, like lightning he struck the king; hear, he rings the alarum; see, he stirs up the people! He is everywhere and nowhere like the devil himself, while all that now stirs is moved by him!

KOLL.

Turn away from him, Tjostulv!

TJOSTULV [*quietly*].

Where is he that hath slain the king?

ALL.

We know not!

HALLKELL.

He comes not in the daylight, he flashes out like an evil thought, he springs like a tiger, he slays like a snake; thus does he come, and thus go!

SEVERAL.

Where is he ?

OTHERS.

Ay, where is he?

ALL.

Where is he ?   Where is he?

IVAR KOLLBEJNSON [*standing on a high rock and looking out upon the fjord*].

Hush !   There is a man in a blue cloak, who calls to us from a boat below.

SIGURD'S VOICE [*slowly*].

Seek you him who hath slain the king ?

THE PEOPLE.

Yes.

SIGURD'S VOICE.

It is I who did it; I, Sigurd Magnusson.

THE PEOPLE.

Then it was he.

IVAR KOLLBEJNSON.

For he had much to avenge.

SIGURD'S VOICE.

I have avenged blind Magnus and myself.   Now we will share the throne together.

THE PEOPLE.

Together !

KOLL *to* [*Hallkell*].

This will win the people!

IVAR KOLLBEJNSON.

Then shall peace quickly come, good people.

THE PEOPLE.

Ay, it is peace that we would have.

SIGURD'S VOICE.

If you accept this deed there shall be peace in the land, and no ill-hap, save one man's death, who should never have been king.

IVAR KOLLBEJNSON.

The first true word I ever heard said of Harald!

MANY.

Yes, yes!

HALLKELL [*to Koll*].

Things are going ill!

IVAR KOLLBEJNSON.

Hush!   [*A pause.*

SIGURD'S VOICE.

Is there no chieftain on the bridge?

MANY VOICES.

Yes; Tjostulv Åleson is here!

SIGURD'S VOICE.

He should have a word for me.   [*All turn to Tjostulv.*

TJOSTULV [*slowly mounts upon a rock*].

Yes; I have a word for thee, Sigurd. Either art thou Harald's brother, when it is clear that thou wert born in sin, or thou art not Harald's brother, and the work thou hast done doubly foul.

SIGURD'S VOICE.

Think of it again, Tjostulv Åleson. Think also of me!

TJOSTULV.

When thou didst plunge the sword in thy brother's breast thou didst forget that the deed would drive me and all honest men from thee.

SIGURD'S VOICE [*very slowly*].

For what I have done I can answer before God.

TJOSTULV.

That may well be, but before me thou canst not answer it. I had given thee aid to the very limit of the law, but now thou callest upon me from without its pale.

SIGURD'S VOICE.

Let come, then, what God will!

TJOSTULV [*to the people*].

Hear! He turns the evil of his mind to the will of God! Thus at the last he will deceive himself, as he has now deceived us. He is a dangerous man, and beneath his fair seeming there lurks a dark purpose. But we will be bound by the law of the land. The children of

Harald now claim its protection, and stretch out their little hands for help. For that man yonder in the blue cloak — cast stones into his boat and drive him from the shore, for he brings ill-fortune with him.

THE PEOPLE.

Yes, yes! Out upon thee, thou murderer of thy brother!

[*They cast stones at him. As Tjostulv descends, Hallkell falls upon his breast, and Koll grasps his hand. Then all draw their swords and lay them together; Sigurd Stallar and Gyrd, who have also entered, lay theirs with the rest.*

ACT FOURTH.

More than two years later. A great cave by the Gljusre Fjord at Tjeldesund. Sails are hung as curtains in the background, so that they can be drawn aside. Ship's tools and skins of animals strewn about the ground.

SCENE FIRST.

IVAR KOLLBEJNSON [*others enter during the scene*].

IVAR [*sewing upon a sheepskin cap. He calls out*].

Has he shot the deer? Then we will have it for dinner. No, may you? God's death! Skin it at once! What? Grouse? I think the very devil is in you! Leave the grouse lying in the snow and skin the deer! [*The sail is drawn aside, revealing an outlook over the majestic landscape ; snow-mountains upon one side and the dark sea upon the other ; moonlight bathes the scene. Three skin-clad men try to enter with a slain deer.*] Don't bring it in until the chieftain comes up from the sea with the stranger! [*They leave.*] Pull the sail to : it is cold here! [*They do as they are bid ; he sews on, muttering all the while to himself.*] Whom are you shouting to? They will not answer now. Who is coming? They pretend not to hear now.

[*The sail is once more drawn aside; a skin-clad man enters.*]

ERLEND.

The chieftain shouts up that they cannot climb any further, the ice is breaking.

IVAR KOLLBEJNSON [*after waiting a little*].

Why dost thou stand there gaping? Take the rope and wind it down!

> [*Erlend takes up a coiled rope and goes; the sail is drawn to again. Ivar Kollbejnson rises, puts things to order, but acts as if weary of solitude.*

SCENE SECOND.

The same. SIGURD SLEMBE, IVAR INGEMUNDSON.

IVAR INGEMUNDSON [*looks first about the cave, then at Ivar Kollbejnson, who evades his glance*].

That is Ivar Kollbejnson!

IVAR KOLLBEJNSON.

H'm!

IVAR INGEMUNDSON.

I have never seen a man grow so old in two years.

IVAR KOLLBEJNSON.

H'm!   [*Goes.*

SIGURD.

Ivar Kollbejnson has outlived many illusions, and the greatest of them last of all.

IVAR INGEMUNDSON.

He must be cold company for you. A whole winter in this Northland cave with him!

SIGURD [*lies down*].

Life does not always bring warmth. It was good of you to come: it is lonesome here.

IVAR INGEMUNDSON [*sits down*].

But what a time I have had in finding you! After
you lost in the last fight I thought Magnus the blind
would seek the cloister.　But he was not there, and so
I looked for him with his old foster father in Bjarkö,
and there I found him.　I am the only one whom he
would tell where you were.

SIGURD.

What do the people think?

IVAR INGEMUNDSON.

The people think that you went down in the last
storms of autumn.

SIGURD.

They think themselves safe now.

IVAR INGEMUNDSON.

Yes, the army has disbanded, and the chieftains gone
home.

SIGURD.

So be it!　But why did you believe that I was living?

IVAR INGEMUNDSON.

There was one who said so with much assurance.

SIGURD.

And yet none might bring any tidings of me.　For
none who for any cause came hither have ever returned.

IVAR.

What mean you?

SIGURD.

What I say. The time for scruples is now past with me. The Finns have given me food. There is nothing to which one may not become used. Five years ago I drank camel's milk with Arabs; this winter, reindeer's milk with Finns.

IVAR.

And you think to maintain this struggle?

SIGURD.

I have a new sort of ships that will outsail all others. The Finns have built them for me. I set out in them to-morrow or the day after, and I shall find the chieftains one by one.

IVAR.

Then you will never desist?

SIGURD.

Yes, when my aim is reached.

IVAR.

But you have now failed for more than two years.

SIGURD.

Say, rather, I have failed for more than seventeen; for it is thus long since I began. Ivar, do you believe that my cause is just? And do you believe that I may achieve something if once I reach the throne of my fathers?

IVAR.

I believe that your right to be king of Norway is

greater than that of any other living man ; I believe that
as king you would build all anew.

SIGURD [*who has risen*].

And you can yet ask if I will desist?

IVAR [*remains sitting*].

I will tell you something of my life, poor compared
with yours, but not without experience, A maiden in
Iceland was so dear to me that I could not bear to
think of a future without her. And yet I said nothing,
not even when I left to sojourn in strange lands. But
once when my brother returned home, I bade him tell
her that she must wait, for I could not live without her.

SIGURD.

She was thy life's aim.

IVAR.

She was mine. When I returned, I went to my
brother's, and there I met her as his wife.

SIGURD.

What didst thou then ?

IVAR.

What would you have done ?

SIGURD.

That I know not.

IVAR.

I will tell you. First you would have left and

returned — twice or so — but you would have slain him.

SIGURD.

No ! That aim would have been too low for me.

IVAR.

But suppose that she meant for you the kingdom of Norway ?   [*Pause.*

SIGURD.

Thou hast never been joyful since.

IVAR.

Would I have been so the more, had I killed my brother ?

SIGURD.

Harald Gille was a wretch, a reptile, who defiled my throne, and sought my own life !

IVAR.

Not he, but his followers.

SIGURD.

The land was lawless, and his the guilt.

IVAR.

Well, let that pass. Do you remember, Sigurd, that you have a mother ?

SIGURD.

Why dost thou ask me that ?

IVAR.

Would you see her — talk with her?

SIGURD.

Dost thou know her?   Where is she?

IVAR.

She was on the bridge at Bergen that night — the last night you were there.   She remained until I came.

SIGURD.

Saint Olaf!

IVAR.

Would you speak with her?

SIGURD.

No!   Later.   No, not now.

IVAR.

Then you are not at peace with yourself?

SIGURD.

Not so; but now we should not understand one another.

IVAR.

Yet it might be so.

SIGURD.

To meet were to bring ill to us both.

IVAR.

Your mother has outlived the time when anything in the world could again bring her ill.

SIGURD.

But she lives ?

IVAR.

Yes. I but meant that she sees in you only her son ; all the rest matters little to her.

SIGURD.

But much to me. One would fain have accomplished something before he again meets his mother.

IVAR.

Your mother is old now.

SIGURD.

Yes, she must be old.

IVAR.

What I meant was that she might have too long to wait.

SIGURD.

Does she greatly wish to see me ?

IVAR.

She lives for nothing else. She has lost her right to the protection of the cloister. For two years, now, she has followed you through the land.

SIGURD.

Lord Jesus !

IVAR.

Will you speak with her ?

SIGURD.

Where is she?

IVAR.

I left her at Möre.

SIGURD.

You have followed her, then?

IVAR.

Yes.

SIGURD [*offering his hand*].

Ivar, wilt thou be my friend?

IVAR.

I cannot, my lord.

SIGURD.

Is it too hard for thee, Ivar?

IVAR.

Yes, my lord; for then I should have to share in your work.

SIGURD.

And that thou canst not do?

IVAR.

No, my lord, no — not as you have begun it — and continued it.

SIGURD.

Then go, Ivar!

IVAR.

But first —

SIGURD.

Go, for thou hast fooled me.

IVAR.

I am sorry for it. But let not your mother for my sake want an answer.

SIGURD.

She shall see me — when I sit upon the throne of Norway.

IVAR.

The poor soul will weep many tears ere that time.

SIGURD.

The burden she bears is no heavier than mine.

IVAR.

But her love is stronger, my lord! She may not so endure delay.

SIGURD.

But ay! for it is so little that she craves.

IVAR.

Yet when you returned, you, too, craved but little.

SIGURD.

Many things have changed since then.

IVAR.

May I say it once more, my lord ? When a man has grown afraid to meet his mother the change is not for the better.

SIGURD.

Afraid ? You have mistaken me. Tell my mother that I will meet her where she will.

IVAR.

It is but pride that forces him to this.

SIGURD.

Name thou the place ; we have no more a home.

IVAR.

If she but speak with you home shall be found again.

SIGURD.

Yes ; but it must be agreed that naught be said of my plans, for you know well that in them I make no changes.

IVAR.

But, my lord, of what else is there to speak ?

SIGURD.

There is enough else, quite enough. But you must tell her this.

IVAR.

She shall be told of it.

SIGURD.

Bear to her my filial greeting, and say that all is well with me.

IVAR.

I will do it.

SIGURD.

Tell her that I hope for a happy outcome.

IVAR.

I will tell her that, also.

SIGURD.

And that all shall be well with her.

IVAR.

If she live.

SIGURD.

Yes, and should she die meanwhile, she will see even better how well I meant it with her. But the way was long, and led over cold, high places, where there was no warm room for meeting. And now, farewell! Because thou hast brought this message from my mother I will ever hold thee dear.

IVAR.

But you have forgotten to name the place.

SIGURD.

Ah, the place! It were better that she should name it.

IVAR.

No.

SIGURD.

Well, then — but it will be hard to find me, for henceforth I go upon uncertain ways.

IVAR.

There are many gray islets along the coast, name one of them, and she shall be there.

SIGURD.

Gray islets, sayest thou ?   Holmengrå !

IVAR.

It is far to the south.

SIGURD.

But just on my way when I sail from Denmark in the summer.

IVAR.

Holmengrå ?

SIGURD.

Yes.   It is quiet in the bay there.

IVAR.

We shall meet.

SIGURD.

Dost thou, too, follow ?

IVAR.

Yes.

SIGURD.

Why art thou, then, so concerned for my mother, yet wilt not be my friend?

IVAR.

I cannot tell you all the reason.

SIGURD.

I have never before prayed for a man's confidence or friendship — and thou deniest me both.

IVAR.

With you it is but as a moment's impulse. Your soul reaches out after higher things.

SIGURD.

But a friend upon the way — one only.

IVAR.

Then set your path so low that I may. Come with me to your mother, send your men to their homes, make an end of it all, weep once with her, and, God in heaven! what friends we shall become!

SIGURD.

Now the skald in you speaks, Ivar, and all the deeds of a lifetime become dissolved in one moment of emotion.

IVAR.

Farewell!

SIGURD [*calling*].

Draw the sail! [*It is done, Ivar goes.*] Farewell! [*Calls.*] Ivar Kollbejnson! [*Ivar enters.*] That man is not to be struck down! Send two men to row him over the fjord, — dost thou understand?

IVAR KOLLBEJNSON.

H'm! [*Goes.*

SCENE THIRD.

SIGURD [*alone*].

He too scorns me! No! No more prayers for friend-ship! No more begging! What have I lost during these two years, through my weakness in seeking to gain friends by mildness! I saw quickly we should not suc-ceed that way, but Magnus would have it so — and now we are cast as a wreck upon the shore, for such is life! Light craft must bear us — swift oars cleave the water, for we row death shorewards. My right is from God, and my sufferings from men; it is for mé now to recon-cile them.

The mighty, in betraying me, have betrayed the land. Therefore shall the land have their bodies, and I their goods. He who has goods has power, and he who has power gets success — friends are needless then. The helmsman prays not for warm sun and calm sea. Rather does he rejoice when the wind begins to whistle in the rigging. [*A woman's voice is heard singing.*

Ah, that is the Finnish maiden calling her dogs. I am glad that she has come. She is like the dawn of life with its dreams and its yearnings. She is like the northern light, streaming with its uncertain gleam over the twilight heavens.   Were the light stronger, it would be colorless.

> [*The sail is raised suddenly: the Finnish maiden appears in the opening.*

SCENE FOURTH.

SIGURD SLEMBE, THE FINNISH MAIDEN.

THE MAIDEN.

I buckled on my snow-shoes and came down the mountain; for is it true that the fires are quenched in the cavern, and that thou steerest once more for thy star?

SIGURD.

Yes.

THE MAIDEN [*stepping forward, with a warning gesture*].

Ah, believe not in it! It has led thee from the land where the sand burns beneath the feet, and hither, where the snow lays its roof upon the tent, — see, how unsafe a guide it is!

SIGURD.

I could not always see it; therefore did I fare so far.

THE MAIDEN.

It leads astray! My father, the old king, has asked the Great Spirit concerning thee, — and we tremble.

SIGURD.

What saw he?

THE MAIDEN.

A battle-field and many slain.

SIGURD [*fearful*].

Was I among them ?

THE MAIDEN.

No.

SIGURD.

Then take comfort, for my way leads over the field.

THE MAIDEN.

Then saw he an island in the sea.   Many men were there in blue garments.   And others came up from the sea and sat down with them.

SIGURD.

Was I among them ?

·THE MAIDEN.

No ! but they who came from the sea were the slain kinsmen of the others, wet and gray, — and they bore with them a bound man.

SIGURD.

Who was he ?

THE MAIDEN.

Thou wert he !   [*Sigurd sits down.*]   Let me sit at thy knee !   [*Sitting at his feet.*]   What is the name of thy God?

SIGURD.

He has no name.

THE MAIDEN.

Where lives he?

SIGURD.

Everywhere.

THE MAIDEN.

Is he here now?

SIGURD.

Surely.

THE MAIDEN.

Then ask him if thy journey shall be fortunate.

SIGURD.

He will not answer me.

THE MAIDEN.

With signs, I mean, and other signs shall answer.

SIGURD.

No, he answers not.

THE MAIDEN.

What is he good for, then?

SIGURD [*pointing to his breast*].

He speaks here, and here bids me loosen the knots I
have tied, and seek the goal that is set me.

THE MAIDEN.

And has he named this goal?

SIGURD.

It was set at my birth and revealed by my fate.

THE MAIDEN.

And this goal is death?

SIGURD.

What sayest thou?

THE MAIDEN.

Thou dost journey but to meet a hard death; thus says the Great Spirit. *[A pause.*

SIGURD.

So my God's will shall be done.

THE MAIDEN.

Then thy God is a hard God!

SIGURD.

Peace!

THE MAIDEN.

No wonder; for all the people who worship Him are hard. They are, like thee, ever unsatisfied. First they took our land in the south, then they took it in the north, and now they have driven us up to the snow. But they forget us not even yet, and each year they come and take the tithe of our possessions. And when they have taken it, they slay one another in strife for it!

SIGURD.

The evil in them is not of God.

THE MAIDEN.

But He speaks in your own breast ! Look at thyself !
Hast thou not told me of thy life's course — has it not
been insatiable as theirs ? Why wouldst thou not stay
with thy mother ? Thou wert well received by a foreign
chieftain, why didst thou leave him ? Didst thou not
serve an earl with honor, why didst thou depart ? Wert
thou not a captain in the far southern lands, and yet
turned thee homewards ? Didst thou not gather ships
and goods upon the sea, what didst thou do with them ?
Now thou art defeated and forsaken by the people of
whom thou art king, and wouldst thou seek them again ?
Is not thy God a hard God, that He pursues thee with
ceaseless unrest, and now drives thee to thy death ?

Look at our people ! No man here owns garments
of foreign wool, or adornments of any kind, but eats his
reindeer's flesh and drinks their milk ; sleeps never save
on the ground, and yields up the tithe of his belongings
to thy people ; has no house save the open air — and
yet we are happy ! For we know that when death shall
bring us over the eternal snow-mountains, there shall
shine a great noble land, where the sun is ever up, and
the brooks have melted the snow; where the birches
grow to threefold height and bear fruit; and where the
Great Spirit shall come down to the shore and draw to
him all the beasts of the forest and the sea, and men
shall walk among them with no evil thoughts. [*She rises.*

Oh, Sigurd, hear me ! I am a Finnish maiden, less
than thou and thy people. But thou didst not come
like other strangers to rob and slay ; my people love

thee, and I may speak thus to thee. Thou hast entered our tents, and sat at our boards; thou hast told us of strange countries, and taught us useful things. See, when thou comest our dogs do not bark, but lick thy hand, and the reindeer rub against thy clothes. Stay with us! My father owns five thousand deer, I am his heir — take half of them, and drive them whither thou wilt! Thy God is everywhere; then He is in the everlasting snow-mountains!

SIGURD.

Once before did a maiden entice me as thou, — and thou art like her.

THE MAIDEN.

And what she offered thee —

SIGURD.

I might not take then, because I sought for greater things. Now —

THE MAIDEN.

Now —

SIGURD.

Now I must be steadfast to the end, not only for my own sake, but for theirs who trust in me.

THE MAIDEN.

Dost thou think it shall go well with thee?

SIGURD.

That I know not. But as things now are, a life among you would be terrible.

THE MAIDEN [*offended*].

Terrible ?

SIGURD.

Rather death itself: all would then be over !

THE MAIDEN [*alarmed*].

Are we worse than death to thee ?

SIGURD.

Thou dost not understand me.

THE MAIDEN.

Tell me what I do not understand !

SIGURD.

There is something dearer to me than all things else. If thou shouldst love a man, wouldst thou not forsake all to follow him ?

THE MAIDEN.

Yes, if he loved me.

SIGURD.

And not otherwise ?

THE MAIDEN.

No !

SIGURD.

Thou wouldst seek to win him ?

THE MAIDEN.

No !

SIGURD.

But then wouldst thou be unhappy.

THE MAIDEN.

For an hour.   But when I came to another clearing, where I might feel myself a child again —

SIGURD.

Couldst thou then forget him ?

THE MAIDEN.

Oh, yes, — if it were summer.

SIGURD.

I cannot explain my meaning to thee.

THE MAIDEN.

May I explain something to thee ?

SIGURD.

Willingly.

THE MAIDEN.

Canst thou feel how fair it is here ?

SIGURD.

Ah, yes, at times.   When I stand outside the cave and see the unending snow, the trees above it seem like mighty spectres warning me in the twilight.   Then thou comest sliding down the mountain upon thy snow-shoes, thy dogs about thee, thy followers behind, and you all seem of threefold stature.   And when the colored streamers of the northern light shine over your path and over all this enchanted fairyland, narrowing, broadening, wildly, weirdly, — yes, then deep feelings take hold of me.

THE MAIDEN.

And what dost thou feel then ?

SIGURD.

Yearnings for all that my life has not reached.

THE MAIDEN [*remains for a time musing : then recovers herself*].

Ah, I understand ; that is because thou hast never seen the summer here. Then wouldst thou have yearnings for naught else.

SIGURD.

But in winter thou too hast yearnings for something else.

THE MAIDEN.

Yes, I yearn for the sun. But in summer it never sets ; I sleep outdoors with my dogs, and the deer lie about. We rest an hour, we wander an hour ; night is as day and day as night ; we think of no future ; it seems as if it would never end, or as if the end of all things were come.

SIGURD.

Then would I yearn the more!

THE MAIDEN.

Then thou canst not know what joy is. Canst thou love a dog ?

SIGURD.

There are times when I can love the smallest thing.

THE MAIDEN [*in wonderment*].

But not always?

SIGURD.

Most often I have no time to think of it.

THE MAIDEN.

No time, what does that mean?

SIGURD.

My eye does not see it.

THE MAIDEN.

Now I understand. [*Starts to go.*

SIGURD.

Wilt thou go? Ah, thou thinkest I cannot bear thy people, thy country!

THE MAIDEN.

More than that! Go thy way!

SIGURD.

Wherefore?

THE MAIDEN.

No spot on earth can give thee rest, and no being lives for whom thou canst care! Thy God must be a hard God, and death dear to thee! Now I understand that thou must depart! Farewell!

SIGURD.

Ah, but stay !

THE MAIDEN.

I will call my deer, strike my tents, and journey
southwards to await the sun !

[*The sail is raised and she disappears.*

SCENE FIFTH.

SIGURD [*alone*].

The snow-flake melts when it falls upon the warm
hand. In an hour I shall have ceased to remember
her.

A man must look beyond his birthplace and his kin ;
they are as forests that shut out our view. What he
may see beyond them is not as fair as he has pictured it,
but he has clearness of vision. His goal appears before
him, and he goes in safety.

Why have I no more following? Why won Harald
Gille friends — and not I? Because I let down no
ladder of weakness for my approach. High upon my
rights I stand ; the law would come to me, but has no
strength to climb ; therefore I am alone.

Pity myself? I, who am come to bring the law ! The
axe cannot be the forest's friend, or the hoe the weed's,
or the huntsman the beast of prey's. Shame and dishonor, should they who loved Harald Gille love me !

SCENE SIXTH.

SIGURD. [*The sail is raised ; skin-clad men enter and fill the cave.*]

SIGURD.

It is noon ?

THE MEN.

Yes !

SIGURD.

Our last here.

THE MEN.

Well !

SIGURD.

You are glad, I see. You long for plunder ? You shall have it. I know that not one of you goes for my sake.

SEVERAL.

Yes, yes !

SIGURD.

Still ! No lies ! It does not matter to me ! [*To Ivar Kollbejnson.*] Dost thou press forward, old man ? Thou hast stood at my side in every fight, thou wilt say, and didst prepare my camp afterwards. H'm ! thou dost but seek revenge upon the strong, and thou dost think that I can best give it thee ! [*Ivar holds out a cap.*] Hast thou made this cap for me ? Hast thou bound up

my wounds this winter? Ay, like the peasant, who
grinds his axe at the hour of noon. Still! No more
lies. I know it. I know, too, that I am held in your
hands as a hawk by a cord; you let me fly that I may
make a capture. You shall have it! I have need of
you; as you are, we suit one another, for we now go
forth to greet all traitors, law-breakers, murderers in
the land. I am the law, for I am the king! I now
decree that every chieftain in the land, every king's
steward, every peasant-leader, who has betrayed Magnus
and me, is doomed to death, and his possessions are
mine! In our light ships we will fall upon them; behind us a burning settlement, and before, one that awaits
us! Then shall we see if many do not flock to our
cause, when it is shown them that something may be
gained by it! And when my strength is great enough,
I will give battle, and thence mount the throne. Then,
at a sign, the fire shall be quenched in the land, and
grain grow once more, and if you obey me not, your
turn shall come. You hear now what bond holds us together, what you have to await, and what to fear. Stand
from me! It is not your love I would have, but your
hatred, your lust for plunder, your thirst for revenge,
that I may use them to kindle the flame. No, cast not
down your heads, care not for me; I am happiest
thus!

ACT FIFTH.

Upon Holmengrå. Ranged by the seashore are high rocks. It is an autumn evening, near sunset, and the sky is clear. Out at sea many long ships may be seen, sailing up.

SCENE FIRST.

GYRD, SIGURD STALLAR, *and* TJOSTULV ÅLESON *enter, climbing up from the beach one after the other.* HALLKELL *and* KOLL *follow, out of breath; they have grown much older in these three years. As they come up they group themselves together and look out to the right. There is long silence among them.*

TJOSTULV [*turning towards the others*].

Well, why are we silent? We cannot hide the fact; here are Sigurd's forces, equal to our own!

HALLKELL.

Three months ago he had two Finnish boats; to-day he has a mighty fleet.

GYRD.

Now I begin to fear. The more we defeat him, with the greater strength does he come against us.

HALLKELL.

I depend upon this: that every third man in our army has a slain kinsman to avenge, — it gives them courage.

TJOSTULV.

Sigurd's men have nothing to lose, and all to gain, and the courage of revenge is equaled by that of the beast of prey.

GYRD.

But the other two thirds of our men fight with the strength of despair.

KOLL.

Who are they, then, who fight for the country?

TJOSTULV.

There are not many such in civil strife.

[*Koll sits down in the middle, and the others follow his example, all but Tjostulv, who looks steadily in the direction of Sigurd's fleet.*

HALLKELL.

Should we lose this fight, God only knows what our fate will be.

GYRD.

We know well enough it will be that of the many chieftains, whose goods he seized, whose houses he burned, and whose bodies had to be cut down from the gallows.

SIGURD STALLAR.

It will be like our brother Bejntejn's.

HALLKELL.

Poor Bejntejn! He took fearful vengeance upon him!

GYRD.

Upon all, upon all!   Harder man was there never in Norway since our people dwelt there.

HALLKELL.

They say that retribution will come upon him.   I do not understand that saying; for one man cannot atone for the death of a hundred.

GYRD.

Yes — if his death be made as lingering as that of a hundred.

KOLL.

No man could bear to see that.

GYRD.

I know of one who could bear it.

SIGURD STALLAR.

And I of one.

TJOSTULV [*looking out on the fleet*].

His ships are larger than ours; we cannot board them. So we have something other to think of than the manner of Sigurd's death.

KOLL.

Thou hast lost courage, Tjostulv?

TJOSTULV

Yes.   I will not conceal the fact that in every battle I have won from him, my strength was the greater.

This time it is not so, — and Sigurd is a better leader than I.

KOLL.

But thou countest the most prows.

TJOSTULV.

No, look for thyself! The evening sun shines on them; thou canst count them.

KOLL.

Wait till the gray of morning, — and thou shalt see the half of them stand out to sea!

ALL.

What sayest thou?

KOLL.

They are Danes and would go home again.

ALL.

Do the Danes desert him?
                [*Hallkell, Gyrd, and Sigurd Stallar jump up.*

KOLL [*remains seated*].

I have had a little boat in among them, and to-morrow at sunrise will they hoist their sails, for they have gained what they sought in Norway.

TJOSTULV.

Then an overwhelming victory awaits us!

HALLKELL.

Hemmed in upon every side —

SIGURD STALLAR *and* GYRD.

He is ours with all his force.

TJOSTULV.

Then let Saint Olaf be praised in all time to come, for from to-morrow the peasant may sleep with open doors.

HALLKELL.

And it is our lot to appoint the solemn hour of judgment.

GYRD.

If it turns out as I hope, the church will have cause to rejoice.

SIGURD STALLAR.

And if it turns out as I wish, the bishop's seat in Stavanger shall have two boatloads of fire-wood; they need it on that bleak rock.

GYRD.

What is thy wish, brother?

SIGURD STALLAR.

What is thine?

GYRD.

Perhaps our wish is the same.

HALLKELL.

You both wish that he may fall alive into your hands.

KOLL.

If it turns out as I wish, I will set two gold candle-sticks in the church that I have built.

TJOSTULV.

What is thy wish, old man?

KOLL.

That he may die like a warrior, — for as such he has lived.

TJOSTULV.

That is my thought also.

HALLKELL.

As a robber and a bloodhound has he lived, — and he must die as such!

SIGURD STALLAR.

That is the thought of the whole host!

GYRD.

And it will fare ill with any one who opposes it!

TJOSTULV.

Hast thou, Koll, ever known a man to be hated thus?

KOLL.

No.

HALLKELL.

But there has never lived before so cold-blooded a murderer. Such a cruise as his last exceeds all known horrors.

GYRD.

Think of how our brother Bejntejn was slain! He hewed off his head, and let the blood drip out among his men.

TJOSTULV [*sits down; the others do likewise*].

Yes; a devil has indeed taken possession of him, and now holds full sway. To no other have I ever been so closely drawn as to Sigurd, and no one has so far repelled me!

HALLKELL.

I was never drawn to him. From the first hour I was forced to use well my strength that I might not fall beneath his heel. It seems to me that none might live near him, save as bondsmen.

TJOSTULV.

That I never felt. There was a time when I would have given him everything, even my life. Who knows? Good fortune might have made him a great king.

KOLL.

I do not believe that. If misfortune turn his disposition to evil, power would but make him hard.

TJOSTULV.

He is one of those men who force all the world to rise up against them, to surround, and to destroy. And when it is done, we stand about regretful.

HALLKELL.

Thou, Koll, hast known him from a child; thou knowest him better than we.

KOLL.

No. But this I will say : that were he again to begin the strife, and I again to counsel him, he should get other than worldly wisdom from me.

When he returned a man, we feared him. It was the strength of his nature that we feared — feared lest it shatter our own designs. Who shall conquer in the end, no one of us may foresee ; at this moment not only has he overturned our work, but the whole country has trembled in his hand.

Of late his own strength has bewitched him. He has heard in nature the echo of evil things, and may no more cease to call upon her. He has come to be such that either must we all take flight, and he alone live, or else the powers that cannot here find fitting exercise must be scattered like vapors.

But this thing I believe, that the powers here but imperfectly revealed in the strife will yonder be gathered together to noble outcome. My friends, I believe in a life after this one.

[*He rises, turns around, and beholds Sigurd, whose head at this moment appears above the rocks. Sigurd is pale as death, and immediately disappears. Koll is startled, but keeps silence.*

TJOSTULV.

It seems to me as if we were the country's doomsmen, and had sat in judgment upon him.

HALLKELL [*rising*].

Since the Danes forsake him, we go not to battle to-morrow, but rather to carry out the country's judgment upon him.

GYRD [*rising with the others*].

And that judgment is that all his men shall fall, and he be captured alive.

KOLL.

Nay! [*With raised voice.*] Could he hear me now, I would tell him to fall at the head of his followers, or to take his own life; for he must not come into the hands of evil men.

TJOSTULV.

God help the man who must put up with such counsel!

SIGURD STALLAR.

It is more than he deserves.

KOLL.

Were God as severe as man, the world would soon be empty. [*Crosses with the others.*

GYRD.

There is a boat moored by ours. [*Looking around.*] There are several.

KOLL.

A fisherman after bait. [*As Gyrd makes an attempt to look down.*] Give me your hand, Gyrd!
[*Gyrd hastens to help him down from the rock.*

SCENE SECOND.

The scene is at first empty. Then SIGURD SLEMBE *enters, climbing over a rock; he comes forward in silence, but powerfully agitated.*

SIGURD.

The Danes forsake me! The battle is lost! Thus far — and no further!

Escape to the mountains to-night! Exchange my ships for freedom! There are herds of horses on the mountains, we will climb up there and then fall upon the valleys like a snow-storm.

But when winter comes? To begin at the beginning; the outlaw's life — never more! I have made my last effort; had it been successful, men would have wondered at me. It has failed, and vengeance is loose. I cannot gather another force in Norway!

All over? Thus far and no further? No! The Danes sail, but we will sail with them! This night, this very night we will raise our yards and follow them to the open sea.

But whither shall we turn our prows? To Denmark? We will raise no third force in Denmark. Start out again as merchant? No! Serve in foreign lands? No! Crusade? No! Hither and no further! Sigurd, the end has come!

[*Almost sobbing.*] Death! The thought sprang up in my mind as a door springs open, clashing upon its hinges; light, air, receive me! [*He draws his sword.*] No, I will fall fighting for the cause I have lived for — my men shall have a leader!

Is there no chance of victory? no trick? Can I not get them ashore? Can I not get them in the toils?

try them in point-blank fight, man to man, all the
strength of despair fighting with me? Ah, could they
but hear me, could I but find some high place and
speak to them; tell them how clear as the sun is my
right, how monstrous the wrongs I have borne, what a
crime is theirs in withstanding me! You murder not
me alone, but thousands upon thousands of thoughts for
my fatherland's welfare; I have carried nothing out,
I have not sown the least grain, or laid one stone upon
another to witness that I have lived. Ah, I have
strength for better things than strife; it was the desire
to work that drove me homewards; it was impatience
that wrought me ill! Believe me, try me, give me but
half what Harald Gille promised me, even less; I ask
but very little, if I may still live and strive to accomplish
something! Jesus, my God, it was ever the little that
thou didst offer me, and that I ever scorned!

Where am I? I stand upon my own grave, and hear
the great bell ring. I tremble as the tower beneath its
stroke, for where now are the aims that were mine?
The grave opens its mouth and makes reply. But life
lies behind me like a dried-up stream, and these eighteen years are lost as in a desert. The sign, the sign
that was with me from my birth! In lofty flight I have
followed it hither with all the strength of my soul, and
here I am struck by the arrow of death; I fall, and behold the rocks beneath upon which I shall be crushed.
Have I, then, seen awrong? Ah, how the winds and currents of my life stood yonder, where it was warm and
fruitful, while I toiled up where it grew ever colder, and
my ship is now clasped by the drifting icebergs; a moment yet and it must sink. Then let it sink, and all
will be over. [*On his knees.*] But in thy arms, All-
merciful, I shall find peace!

What miracle is this? For in the hour I prayed the prayer was granted! Peace, perfect peace! [*Rises.*] Then will I go to-morrow to my last battle as to the altar; peace shall at last be mine for all my longings.

> [*Holds his head bowed and covered by his hands. As he, after a time, slowly removes them, he looks around.*

How this autumn evening brings reconciliation to my soul! Sun and wave and shore and sea flow all together, as in the thought of God all others; never yet has it seemed so fair to me! Yet it is not mine to reign over this lovely land. How greatly I have done it ill! But how has it all come so to pass? for in my wanderings I saw thy mountains in every sky, I yearned for home as a child longs for Christmas, yet I came no sooner, and when at last I came — I gave thee wound upon wound.

But thou, in contemplative mood, now gazest upon me, and givest me at parting this fairest autumn night of thine. I will ascend yonder rock and take a long farewell. [*Mounts up.*

And even thus I stood eighteen years ago, — thus looked out upon the sea, blue beneath the rising sun. The fresh breezes of morning seemed wafted to me from a high future; through the sky's light veil a vision of strange lands was mine; in the glow of the morning sun wealth and honor shone upon me; and to all this, the white sails of the crusaders should swiftly bear me.

Farewell, dreams of my youth! Farewell, my sweet country! Ah, to what sorrows thou hast brought me forth! But now it will soon be over. [*He descends.*

If these ships should sail up to me this very night bearing the fulfillment of all my dreams! Could any one of them be now in truth mine, — or may a tree bear fruit twice in one year?

I give way to make room for some better man. But be Thou gracious to me, and let death be mine with these feelings in my heart, for strength to be faithful might not long be vouchsafed me.

Thou shalt die to-morrow! How sure a father-confessor is that word. Now for the first time I speak truth to myself.

SCENE THIRD.

SIGURD SLEMBE, IVAR INGEMUNDSON *with* THE NUN.

IVAR [*climbing over a rock*].

Yes, here he is. - [*Gives his hand to the nun.*

THE NUN [*without seeing*].

Sigurd! [*Mounts up.*] Yes, there he is!

SIGURD.

Mother!

THE NUN.

My child, found once more! [*They remain long clasped in each other's arms.*] My son, my son, now shalt thou no more escape me!

SIGURD.

Oh, my mother!

THE NUN.

Thou wilt keep away from this battle, is it not so? We two will win another kingdom, — a much better one.

SIGURD.

I understand thee, mother.

[*Leads her to a seat, and falls upon his knee.*

THE NUN.

Yes, dost thou not? Thou art not so bad as all men would have it. I knew that well, but wanted so much to speak with thee, — and since thou art wearied and hast lost thy hopes for this world, thou hast come back to me, for even now there is time! And of all thy realm they must leave thee some little plot, and there we will live by the church, so that when the bells ring for vespers we shall be near the blessed Olaf, and with him seek the presence of the Almighty. And there we will heal thy wounds with holy water, and thoughts of love, more than thou canst remember ever to have had, shall come back to thee robed in white, and wondering recollection shall have no end. For the great shall be made small and the small great, and there shall be questionings and revelations and eternal happiness. Thou wilt come and thus live with me, my son, wilt thou not? Thou wilt stay from this battle and come quickly?

SIGURD.

Mother, I have not wept till now since I lay upon the parched earth of the Holy Land.

THE NUN.

Thou wilt follow me?

SIGURD.

To do thus were to escape the pledges I have made but by breaking them.

THE NUN.

To what art thou now pledged!

SIGURD.

Pledged to the blind king I took from the cloister; pledged to the men I have led hither.

THE NUN.

And these pledges thou shalt redeem — how?

SIGURD.

By fighting and falling at their head.

THE NUN [*springs to her feet. Sigurd also rises*].

No! No! No! Shall I now, after a lifetime of sorrow, behold thy death?

SIGURD.

Yes, mother. The Lord of life and death will have it so.

THE NUN.

Ah! what sufferings a moment's sin may bring! [*She falls upon his breast, then sinks with outstretched arms.*] Oh, my son, spare me!

SIGURD.

Do not tempt me, mother!

THE NUN.

Hast thou taken thought of what may follow? Hast thou thought of capture, of mutilation?

SIGURD.

I have some hymns left me from childhood. I can sing them.

THE NUN.

But I — thy mother — spare me !

SIGURD.

Make not to me this hour more bitter than death itself.

THE NUN.

But why now die ?   We have found one another.

SIGURD.

We two have nothing more to live for.

THE NUN.

Wilt thou soon leave me ?

SIGURD.

Till the morning sun appear we will sit together. Let me lift thee upon this rock. [*He does so and casts himself at her feet.*] It was fair that thou shouldst come to me. All my life is now blotted out, and I am a child with thee once more. And now we will seek out together the land of our inheritance. I must away for a moment to take my leave, and then I shall be ready, and I think that thou, too, art ready.

IVAR INGEMUNDSON [*falling on his knee*].

My lord, now let me be your friend.

SIGURD [*extending his hand*].

Ivar, thou wilt not leave her to-morrow ?

IVAR INGEMUNDSON.

Not until she is set free.

SIGURD.

And now sing me the crusader's song. I may joy-
fully go hence after that.

IVAR INGEMUNDSON [*rises and sings*].

Fair is the earth,
Fair is God's heaven,
Fair is the pilgrim-path of the soul.
Singing we go
Through the fair realms of earth,
Seeking the way to our heavenly goal.

Races shall come,
And shall pass away,
And the world from age to age shall roll ;
But the heavenly tones
Of our pilgrim song
Shall echo still in the joyous soul.

First heard of shepherds,
By angels sung,
Wide it has spread since that glad morn:
Peace upon earth !
Rejoice, all men,
For unto us is a Saviour born.

[*The mother places both her hands on Sigurd's head, and they
look into one another's eyes, he then rests his head upon her
breast.*

TRANSLATOR'S NOTES.

PAGE 3. *Bjarm'land.*

BJARMELAND is often mentioned in the Norse sagas as lying far to the north. Probably the country about the White Sea.

PAGE 3. *Thing.*

The popular assembly of early times in the North. The name is still preserved, although the assemblies have become representative. Thus, in Norway to-day, the legislative body is known as the Storthing, and its two divisions as Lagthing and Odelsthing, respectively.

PAGE 4. *Saint John's Fire.*

The custom of kindling bonfires on Saint John's, or mid-summer eve (June 23), is still kept up in Norway. The practice is of the remotest antiquity.

PAGE 4. *Micklegarth.*

Myklegard, the great city, was the old Norse name for Constantinople. In giving to this word the English form of Micklegarth, the translator has followed Professor E. W. Gosse, in his tragedy of " King Erik."

PAGE 12. *Saint Olaf's Law.*

Olaf II., who consolidated the kingdom of Norway and converted the land to Christianity, reigned from 1015 to

1028. In the latter year, disaffection among his subjects, and the invasion of Knut (Canute the Great), King of Denmark and England, caused Olaf to flee to Russia. In 1030, he returned to Norway at the head of an army and gave battle to Knut at Stiklestad. Having fallen in this battle, his remains were conveyed to the cathedral at Throndhjem, and there interred. In the following century he was proclaimed patron saint of Norway. According to the law as established by him, illegitimacy of birth could not stand in the way of succession to the throne.

PAGE 13.   *The Ordeal.*

The "jærnbyrd," or ordeal here referred to, is the one so familiar to the student of mediæval history, and consisted either in handling a red-hot iron, or in walking barefoot over red-hot plowshares. If, at the end of a certain number of days, the wounds healed without causing any permanent injury, the cause of the person placed upon trial was declared to be just.

PAGE 14.   *King Jorsalfarer.*

Sigurd I. of Norway, who reigned from 1103 to 1130, was named "Jorsalfarer," or "Jerusalem-farer," from the famous expedition made by him in the years 1107–1111. He went by sea to the Holy Land, and thence to Constantinople, doing battle with the heathen in Spain, Portugal, the Balearic Islands, and Palestine. He returned home by land with the remnant of his followers.

PAGE 16.   *Since when the sun grew dark, etc.*

Tradition reports an obscuration of the sun on the day that Olaf fell at Stiklestad. Astronomical calculations show that a total eclipse of the sun occurred in Norway on the 31st of August, 1030. July 29th is, however, the date which tradition assigns to the battle.

PAGE 18. *Chorus of Crusaders.*

Björnson has borrowed the words of this song from the Danish poet and novelist, B. S. Ingemann. A slight alteration has been made in the text.

PAGE 125. *Fafner's Gold.*

Fafner is the giant of Nibelungen tradition. The story of the gold, which brought a curse upon its possessors, has been made familiar to everybody by the Nibelungen tetralogy of Richard Wagner.

PAGE 138. *The Golden-haired Astrid.*

Astrid was the daughter of the King of Sweden, and Olaf married her in opposition to her father's will.

PAGE 219. *Frostathing.*

The Thing held upon the peninsula of Frosta, near Throndhjem. Nidaros was the old name for Throndhjem.

PAGE 288. *Holmengrå.*

There is a play upon words here, based on the fact that "gray islet" is the literal meaning of Holmengrå.

www.ingramcontent.com/pod-product-compliance
Lightning Source LLC
Chambersburg PA
CBHW020946030726
47496CB00005B/1377